Small Ceremonies

Carol Shields

G.K. Hall & Co. • Chivers Press
Thorndike, Maine USA   Bath, Avon, England

This Large Print edition is published by G.K. Hall & Co., USA and by Chivers Press, England.

Published in 1996 in the U.S. by arrangement with Viking Penguin, a division of Penguin Books USA.

Published in 1996 in the U.K. by arrangement with Fourth Estate Limited.

U.S. Hardcover 0-7838-1830-0 (Core Collection Edition)
U.K. Hardcover 0-7451-4926-X (Chivers Large Print)
U.K. Softcover 0-7451-4927-8 (Camden Large Print)

The author wishes to thank the Canada Council for generous support in the writing of this novel.

The text of this Large Print edition is unabridged.
Other aspects of the book may vary from the original edition.

Set in 16 pt. Century Schoolbook by Juanita Macdonald.

Printed in the United States on permanent paper.

British Library Cataloguing in Publication Data available

Library of Congress Cataloging in Publication Data

Shields, Carol.
   Small ceremonies / Carol Shields.
     p.   cm.
   ISBN 0-7838-1830-0 (lg. print : hc)
   1. College teachers' spouses — Ontario — Fiction.
2. Women biographers — Ontario — Fiction. 3. Ontario — Fiction. 4. Large type books. I. Title.
[PR9199.3.S514S43 1996b]
813'.54—dc20   96-19298

For Inez
1902–1971

September

Sunday Night. And the thought strikes me that I ought to be happier than I am.

We have high tea on Sunday, very Englishy, the four of us gathered in the dining ell of our cream-coloured living room at half-past five for cold pressed ham, a platter of tomatoes and sliced radishes. Slivers of hardboiled egg. A plate of pickles.

The salad vegetables vary with the season. In the summer they're larger and more varied, cut into thick peasant slices and drenched with vinegar and oil. And in the winter, in the pale Ontario winter, they are thin, watery, and tasteless, though their exotic pallor gives them a patrician presence. Now, since it is September, we are eating tomatoes from our own suburban garden, brilliant red under a scatter of parsley. Delicious, we all agree.

"Don't we have any mustard?" my husband Martin asks. He is an affectionate and forgetful man, and on weekends made awkward by leisure.

"We're all out," I tell him, "but there's chutney. And a little of that green relish."

"Never mind, Judith. It doesn't matter."

"I'll get the chutney for you," Meredith offers.

"No, really. It doesn't matter."

"Well, I'd like some," Richard says.

"In that case you can just go and get it yourself," Meredith tells him. She is sixteen; he is twelve. The bitterness between them is variable but always present.

Meredith makes a sweep for the basket in the middle of the table. "Oh," she says happily, "fresh rolls."

"I like garlic bread better," Richard says. He is sour with love and cannot, will not, be civil.

"We had that last Sunday," Meredith says, helping herself to butter. Always methodical, she keeps track of small ceremonies.

For us, Sunday high tea is a fairly recent ceremony, a ritual brought back from England where we spent Martin's sabbatical year. We are infected, all four of us, with a surrealistic nostalgia for our cold, filthy flat in Birmingham, actually homesick for fog and made edgy by the thought of swerving red buses.

And high tea. A strange hybrid meal, a curiosity at first, it was what we were most often invited out to during our year in England. We visited Martin's colleagues far out in the endless bricked-up suburbs, and drank cups and cups of milky tea and ate ham and cold beef so thin on the platter it looked almost spiritual. The chirpy wives and their tranquil pipe-sucking husbands, acting out of some inflational good will, drew us into cozy sitting rooms hung with water colours, rows of Penguins framing the gasfires, night pressing in at the windows, so that snugness made us peaceful and generous. Always afterward, driving back to the flat in our little green Austin, we spoke to each other with unaccustomed charity, Martin humming and Meredith exclaiming again and again from the back seat how lovely the Blackstones were and wasn't she, Mrs. Blackstone, a pet.

So we carry on the high tea ritual. But we've never managed to capture that essential shut-in coziness, that safe-from-the-storm solidarity. We fly off in midair. Our house, perhaps, is too open, too airy, and then again we are not the same people we were then; but still we persist.

After lemon cake and ice cream, we move into the family room to watch television. September is the real beginning of the year; even the media know, for the new fall television series are beginning this week.

I know it is the beginning because I feel the wall of energy, which I have allowed to soften with the mercury, toughen up. Get moving, Judith, it says. Martin knows it. All children know it. The first of January

9

is bogus, frosty hung-over weather, a red herring in mindless snow. Winter is the middle of the year; spring the finale, and summer is free; in this climate, at least, summer is a special dispensation, a wave of weather, timeless and tax-free, when heat piles up in corners, sending us sandalled and half-bare to improbable beaches.

September is the real beginning and, settling into our favourite places, Martin and I on the sofa, Meredith in the old yellow chair and Richard stretched on the rug, we sit back to see what's new.

Six-thirty. A nature program is beginning, something called "This Feathered World." The life cycle of a bird is painstakingly described; eggs crack open emitting wet, untidy wings and feet; background music swells. There are fantastic migrations and speeds beyond imagining. Nesting and courtship practices are performed. Two storks are seen clacking their beaks together, bang, slash, bang, deranged in their private frenzy. Richard wants to know what they are doing.

"Courting." Martin explains shortly.

"What's that?" Richard asks. Surely he knows, I think.

"Getting acquainted," Martin answers. "Now be quiet and watch."

We see an insane rush of feathers. A windmill of wings. A beating of air.

"Was that it?" Richard asks. "That was courting?"

"Idiot," Meredith addresses him. "And I can't see. Will you kindly remove your feet, Richard."

"It's a dumb program anyway," Richard says and, rolling his head back, he awaits confirmation.

"It's beautifully done, for your information," Meredith tells him. She sits forward, groaning at the beauty of the birds' outstretched wings.

A man appears on the screen, extraordinarily intense, speaking in a low voice about ecology and the doomed species. He is leaning over, and his hands, very gentle, very sensitive, attach a slender identification tag to the leg of a tiny bird. The bird shudders in his hand, and unexpectedly its ruby throat puffs up to make an improbable balloon. "I'd like to stick a pin in that," Richard murmurs softly.

The man talks quietly all the time he strokes the little bird. This species is rare, he explains, and becoming more rare each year. It is a bird of fixed habits, he tells us; each year it finds a new mate.

Martin, his arm loose around my shoulder, scratches my neck. I lean back into a nest of corduroy. A muscle somewhere inside me tightens. Why?

Every year a new mate; it is beyond imagining. New feathers to rustle, new beaks to bang, new dense twiggy nests to construct and agree upon. But then birds are different from human beings, less individual. Scared little bundles of bones with instinct blurring their small differences; for all their clever facility they are really rather stupid things.

I can hear Meredith breathing from her perch on the yellow chair. She has drawn up her knees and is sitting with her arms circled round them. I can see the delicate arch of her neck. "Beautiful. Beautiful," she says.

I look at Martin, at his biscuity hair and slightly sandy skin, and it strikes me that he is no longer a young man. Martin Gill. Doctor Gill. Associate Professor of English, a Milton specialist. He is not, in fact, in any of the categories normally set aside for the young, no longer a young intellectual or a young professor or a young socialist or a young father.

And we, I notice with a lazy loop of alarm, we are no longer what is called a young couple.

Making the beds the next morning, pulling up the unbelievably heavy eiderdowns we brought back with us from England, I listened to local announcements on the radio. There was to be a "glass blitz" organized by local women, and the public was being asked to sort their old bottles by colour — clear, green and brown — and to take them to various stated depots, after which they would be sent to a factory for recycling.

The organizers of the blitz were named on the air: Gwen Somebody, Peg Someone, Sue, Nan, Dot, Pat. All monosyllabic, what a coincidence! Had they noticed, I wondered. The distance I sometimes sensed between myself and other women saddened me, and I lay flat on my bed for a minute thinking about it.

Imagine, I thought, sitting with friends one day, with Gwen, Sue, Pat and so on, and someone suddenly bursting out with, "I know what. Let's have a glass blitz." And then rolling into action, setting to work phoning the newspapers, the radio stations. Having circulars printed, arranging trucks. A multiplication of committees, akin to putting on a war. Not that I was unsympathetic to the cause, for who dares spoof ecology these days, but what I can never understand is the impulse that actually gets these women, Gwen, Sue, Pat and so on, moving.

Nevertheless, I made a mental note to sort out the bottles in the basement. Guilt, guilt.

And then I got down to work myself at

the card table in the corner of our bedroom where I am writing my third biography.

This book is one that promises to be more interesting than the other two put together, although my first books, somewhat to my astonishment, were moderately well received. The press gave them adequate coverage, and Furlong Eberhardt, my old friend and the only really famous person I know, wrote a long and highly flattering review for a weekend newspaper. And although the public hadn't rushed out to buy in great numbers, the publishers — I am still too self-conscious a writer to say *my* publishers — Henderson and Yeo, had seemed satisfied. Sales hadn't been bad, they explained, for biography. Not everyone, after all, was fascinated by Morris Cardiff, first barrister in Upper Canada, no matter how carefully researched or how dashingly written. The same went for Josephine Macclesfield, prairie suffragette of the nineties.

The relative success of the two books had led me, two years ago, into a brief flirtation with fiction, a misadventure which cost me a year's work and much moral deliberation. In the end, all of it, one hundred execrable pages, was heaved in the wastebasket. I try not to think about it.

I am back in the good pastures of biography now, back where I belong, and in

Susanna Moodie I believe I have a subject with somewhat wider appeal than the other two. Most people have at least heard of her, and thus her name brings forth the sweet jangle of familiarity. Furthermore Susanna has the appeal of fragility for, unlike Morris Cardiff, she was not the first anything and, unlike Josephine, she was not aflame with conviction. She has, in fact, just enough neuroses to make her interesting and just the right degree of weakness to make me feel friendly toward her. Whereas I had occasionally found my other subjects terrifying in their single-mindedness, there is a pleasing schizoid side to Susanna; she could never make up her mind what she was or where she stood.

The fact is, I am enamoured of her, and have felt from the beginning of my re-search, the pleasant shock of meeting a kindred spirit. Her indecisiveness wears well after the rough, peremptory temper of Josephine. Also, she has one of the quali-ties which I totally lack and, therefore, admire, that of reticence. Quaint Victorian restraint. Violet-tinted reserve, stemming as much from courtesy as from decorum.

Decency shimmers beneath her prose, and one senses that here is a woman who hesitates to bore her reader with the idle slopover of her soul. No one, she doubtless argued in her midnight heart, could possibly be interested in the detailing of her rancid sex life or the nasty discomfort of pregnancy in the backwoods. Thus she is genteel enough not to dangle her shredded placenta before her public, and what a lot she resisted, for it must have been a temptation to whine over her misfortunes. Or to blurt out her rage against the husband who brought her to the Ontario wilderness, gave her a rough shanty to live in, and then proceeded into debt; what wonders of scorn she might have heaped on him. One winter they lived on nothing but potatoes; what lyrical sorrowing she might have summoned on that subject. And how admirable of her not to crow when her royalty cheques came in, proclaiming herself the household saviour, which indeed she was in the end. But of all this, there is not one word.

Instead she presents a stout and rubbery persona, that of a generous, humorous woman who feeds on anecdotes and random philosophical devotions, sucking what she can out of daily events, the whole of her life glazed over with a neat edge-to-edge surface. It is the cracks in the surface I look for; for if her reticence is attractive, it also makes her a difficult subject to possess. But who, after all, could sustain such a portrait over so many pages without leaving a few chinks in the varnish? Already

I've found, with even the most casual sleuthing, small passages in her novels and backwoods recollections of unconscious self-betrayal, isolated words and phrases, almost lost in the lyrical brushwork. I am gluing them together, here at my card table, into a delicate design which may just possibly be the real Susanna.

What a difference from my former subject Josephine Macclesfield who, shameless, showed every filling in her teeth. Ah she had an opinion on every bush and shrub! Her introspection was wide open, a field of potatoes; all I had to do was wander over it at will and select the choice produce. Poor Josephine, candid to a fault; I had not respected her in the end. Just as I had had reservations when reading the autobiography of Bertrand Russell who, in passages of obsessive self-abasement, confessed to boyhood masturbation and later to bad breath. For though I forgive him his sour breath and his childhood excesses, it is harder to forgive the impulse which makes it public. Holding back, that is the brave thing.

My research, begun last winter, is going well, and already I have a lovely stack of five-by-seven cards covered with notations. It is almost enough. My old portable is ready with fresh ribbon, newly conditioned at Simpson-Sears. It is ten o'clock; half the morning is gone. Richard will be home from school at noon. I must straighten my shoulders, take a deep breath and begin.

Far away downstairs the back door slammed. "Where are you?" Richard called from the kitchen.

"Upstairs," I answered. "I'll be right down."

At noon Martin eats at the university faculty club, and Meredith takes her lunch to school, so it is only Richard and I for lunch, a usually silent twosome huddled over sandwiches in the kitchen. Today I heated soup and made cheese sandwiches while Richard stood silently watching me. "Any mail?" he asked at last.

"In the hall."

"Anything for me?"

"Isn't there always something for you on Mondays?"

"Not always," he countered nervously.

"Almost always."

Richard dived into the hall and came back with his airletter. He opened it with a table knife, taking enormous care, for he knows from experience that an English airletter is a puzzle of folds and glued edges.

While we ate, sitting close to the brotherly flank of the refrigerator, he read his letter, cupping it toward him cautiously so I couldn't see.

"Don't worry," I chided him. "I'm not going to peek."

"You might," he said, reading on.

"Do you think I've nothing to do but read my son's mail?" I asked, forcing my voice into feathery lightness.

He looked up in surprise. I believe he thinks that is exactly the case: that I have great vacant hours with nothing to do but satisfy my curiosity about his affairs.

In appearance Richard is somewhat like Martin, the same bran-coloured hair, lots of it, tidy shoulders, slender. He will be of medium height, I think, like Martin; and like his father, too, he speaks slowly and with deliberation. For most of his twelve years he has been an easy child to live with; we absorb him unthinking into ourselves, for he is so willingly one of us, so generally unprotesting. At school in England, when Meredith raged about having to wear school uniforms, he silently accepted shirt, tie, blazer, even the unspeakable short pants, and was transformed before our eyes into a boy who looked like someone else's son. And where Meredith despised most of her English schoolmates for being uppity and affected, he scarcely seemed to notice the difference between the boys he played soccer with in Birmingham and those he skated with at home. He is so healthy. The day he was born, watching his lean little arms struggle against the blanket, I gave up smoking forever. Nothing must hurt him.

Absorbed, he chewed a corner of his sandwich and read his weekly letter from Anita Spading, whom he has never met.

She is twelve years old too, and it was her parents, John and Isabel Spalding, who sublet their Birmingham flat to us when we were in England. The arrangements had been made by the university, and the Spaldings, spending the year at the English School in Nicosia, far far away in sunny Cyprus, left us their rambling, freezing and inconvenient flat for which we paid, we later found out, far too much.

To begin with our feelings toward them were neutral, but we began to dislike them the day after we moved in, interpreting our various disasters as the work of their deliberate hands. The rusted taps, the burnt-out lights, the skin of mildew on the kitchen ceiling, a dead mouse in the pantry, the terrible iciness of their lumpy beds; all were linked in a plot to undermine us. Where was the refrigerator, we suddenly asked. How is it possible that there is no heat at all in the bathroom? Fleas in the armchairs as well as the beds?

Isabel we imagined as a slattern in a greasy apron, and John we pictured as a very small man with a tiny brain pickled

20

in purest white vinegar. Its sour workings curdled in his many tidy lists and in the exclamatory pitch of his notes to us. "May I trust you to look after my rubber plant? It's been with me since I took my degree." "You'll find the stuck blind a deuced bother." "The draught from the lavatory window can be wretched, I fear, but we take comfort that the air is fresh." Even Martin took to cursing him. (These days I find it harder to hate him. I try not to think of John Spalding at all, but when I do it is with uneasiness. And regret.)

If nothing else the Spaldings' flat had plenty of bedrooms, windy cubicles really, each equipped like a hotel room with exactly four pieces; bed, bureau, wardrobe and chair, all constructed in cheap utilitarian woods. It was on a bare shelf in his wardrobe that Richard discovered Anita's letter of introduction.

He came running with it into the kitchen where we stood examining the ancient stove. At that time he was only nine, not yet given to secrecy, and he handed the letter proudly to Martin.

"Look what I've found."

Martin read the letter aloud, very solemnly pronouncing each syllable, while the rest of us stood listening in a foolish smiling semicircle. It was a curious note, written in a puckered, precocious style with Lewis

Carroll overtones, but sincere and simple.

To Whoever is the Keeper of This Room,

Greetings and welcome. I am distressed thinking about you, for my parents have told me that you are Canadians which I suppose is rather like being Americans. I am worried that you may find the arrangements here rather queer since I have seen packs and packs of American films and know what kind of houses they live in. This bed, for instance, is rotten through and through. It is odd to think that someone else will actually be sleeping in my bed. But then I shall be sleeping in someone else's bed in Nicosia. They are a Scottish family and they will spend the year in Glasgow, probably in someone else's flat. And the Glasgow family, they'll have to go off and live somewhere, won't they? Isn't it astonishing that we should all be sleeping in one another's beds. A sort of roundabout almost. Whoever you are, if you should happen to be a child (I am nine and a girl) perhaps you would like to write me a letter. I would be delighted to reply. I am exceedingly fond of writing letters but have no connections at the moment.

So please write. Isn't the kitchen a fright! Not like the ones in the films at all.

Your obedient servant,
ANITA DREW SPALDING 9

It took Richard more than a month to write back, although I reminded him once or twice. He hates writing letters, and was busy with other things; I did not press him.

But one dark chilly Sunday afternoon he asked me for some paper, and for an hour he sat at the kitchen table scratching away, asking me once whether there was an "e" in homesick; his or hers, we never knew, for he didn't offer to show us what he'd written. He sealed it shyly, and the next day took it to the post office and sent it on its way to Cyprus.

Anita's reply was almost instantaneous. "It's from her," he explained, showing us the envelope. "From that Cyprus girl." That evening he asked for more paper.

Once a week, sometimes twice, a thick letter with the little grey Cyprus stamp shot through our mail slot. At least as often Richard wrote back, walking to the post office next to MacFisheries at the end of our road in time for the evening pickup.

We never did meet the Spaldings. We left England a month before they returned. We thought Richard would be heartbroken that he would not see Anita, but he seemed not to care much, and I had the idea that the correspondence might drop off when he got home to Canada. But their letters came and went as frequently as ever and seemed to grow even thicker. Postage mounted up, draining off Richard's pocket money, so they switched occasionally to airletters. Always when Richard opens them, he smiles secretly to himself.

"What on earth do you write about?" I asked him.

"Just the same stuff everyone writes in letters," he dodged.

"You mean just news? Like what you've been doing in school?"

"Sort of yeah. Sometimes she sends cartoons from *Punch*. And I send her the best ones out of your old *New Yorkers*."

I find it curious. I don't write to my own sister in Vancouver more than four times a year. To my mother in Scarborough I write a dutiful weekly letter, but sometimes I have to sit for half an hour thinking up items to fill one page. Martin's parents write weekly from Montreal, his mother using one side of the page, his father the other, but even they haven't the stamina of these two mysterious children. Richard's constancy in this correspondence seems oddly serious and out of proportion to childhood, causing me to wonder sometimes whether this little witch in England hasn't got hold of a corner of his soul and somehow transformed it. He is bewitched. I can see it by the way he is sitting here in the kitchen folding her letter. He has read it twice and now he is folding it. Creasing its edges. With tenderness.

"Well, how is Anita these days?" My light voice again.

"Fine." Noncommittal.

"Has she ever sent a picture of herself?"

"No," he says, and my heart leaps. She is ugly.

"Why not?" I ask foxily. "I thought pen-pals always exchanged pictures."

"We decided not to," he says morosely, wincing, or so I believe, at the word pen-pal. Then he adds, "It was an agreement we made. Not to send pictures."

Of course. Their correspondence, I perceive, is a formalized structure, no snapshots, no gifts at Christmas, no postcards ever. Rules in acid, immovable, a pact bound on two sides, a covenant. I can't resist one more question.

"Does she still sign her letters 'your obedient servant?' "

"No," Richard says, and he sighs. The heaviness of that sound tells me that he sighs with love. My heart twists for him. I know the signs, or at least I used to.

Absurd it may be, but I believe it; Richard is as deeply in love at twelve as many people are in a lifetime.

The house we live in — Martin, the children and I — is not really my house. That is, it is not the kind of house I once imagined I might be the mistress of. We live in the suburbs of a small city; our particular division is called Greenhills, and it is neither a town nor a community, not a neighbourhood, not even a postal zone. It is really nothing but the extension of a developer's pencil, the place on the map where he planned to plunk down his clutch of houses and make his million. I suppose he had to call it something, and perhaps he thought Greenhills was catchy and good for sales; or perhaps, who knows, it evoked happy rural images inside his head.

We are reached in the usual way by a main arterial route which we leave and enter by numbered exits and entrances. Greenhills is the seventh exit from the city centre which means we are within a mile or two of open countryside, although it might just as well be ten.

Where we live there are no streets, only crescents, drives, circles and one self-conscious boulevard. It is leafy green and safe for children; our lawns stretch luscious as flesh to the streets; our shrubs and borders are watered.

As soon as the sewers were installed nine years ago, we moved in. The house itself has all the bone-cracking clichés of Sixties domestic architecture: there is a family room, a dining ell, a utility room, a master bedroom with bath *en suite*. A Spanish step-saving kitchen with pass-through, colonial door, attached garage, sliding patio window, split-level grace, spacious garden. The only item we lack is a set of Westminster chimes; the week we moved in, Martin disconnected the mechanism with a screwdriver and installed a doorknocker instead, proving what I have always known, that despite his socialism, he is 90 per cent an aristocrat.

It is a beige and uninteresting house. Curtains join rugs, rugs join furniture; nubby sofa sits between matching lamps on twin tables, direct from Eaton's show room. Utilitarian at the comfort level, there is nothing unexpected. This is a shell to live in without thought.

And in a way it is deliberate, this minimal approach to decorating. My sister Charleen and I, now that we are safely grown up, agree on one thing, and that is that as children we were cruelly overburdened with interior decoration. The house in which we grew up in Scarborough — the old Scarborough that is, before television, before shopping centres, the Scarborough of neat and faintly rural streets — that tiny house was in a constant state of re-vitalization. All our young lives, or so it seemed, we dodged stepladders, stepped carefully around the wet paint, shared the lunch table with wallpaper samples. Our little living room broke out with staggered garlands one year, with French stripes the next, and our girlish bedroom at the back of the house was gutted almost annually. Shaking his head, our father used to say that the rooms would grow gradually smaller under their layers and layers of paint and paper. We would be pushed out on to the street one day, he predicted. It was his little joke, almost his only joke, but straining to recall his voice, do I now hear or imagine the desperate edge? *Better Homes and Gardens* was centred on our coffee table, cheerful with new storage ideas or instructions for gluing bold fabric to attic ceilings. The dining table was in the basement being refinished, or the ches-terfield was being fitted for slipcovers. The pictures were changed with the seasons. "My house is my hobby," Mother used to say to the few visitors we ever had; and even as she spoke, her eyes turned inward, tuned to the next colour scheme, to the ultimate arrangement, just out of reach, beamed in from *House and Garden*, a world the rest of us never entered. Nor wished to.

Still we have put our mark on this place, Martin and I. The floor tiles rise periodically, reminding us they are now nine years old. The utility room is so filled with ski equipment that we call it the ski room. The dining ell has been partitioned off with a plywood planter which looks tacky and hellish, though we thought it a good idea at the time. Hosiery drips from the shower rail in the *en suite* bathroom. In the cool dry basement our first married furniture glooms around the furnace, its Lurex threads as luminous and accusing as the day we bought it; Richard's electric train tunnels between the brass-tipped legs. The spacious garden is the same flat rectangle it always was except for a row of tomato plants and a band of marigolds by the fence.

The house that I once held half-shaped in my head was old, a nook-and-cranny house with turrets and lovely sensuous lips of gingerbread, a night-before-Christmas house, bought for a song and priceless on today's market. Hung with the work of Quebec weavers, an eclectic composition of Swedish and Canadiana. Tasteful but offhand. A study, beamed, for Martin and a workroom, sunny, for me. Studious corners where children might sit and sip their souls in pools of filtered light. A garden drunk with roses, crisscrossed with paths, moist, shady, secret.

This place, 62 Beaver Place, is not really me, I used to say apologetically back in the days when I actually said such things. "We're just roosting here until something 'us' turns up."

I never say it now. If we wanted to, Martin and I could look in his grey file drawer next to his desk in the family room. Between the folders for Tax and Health, we would find House, and from there we could pluck out our offer-to-purchase, the blueprints, the lot survey, the mortgage schedule and, clipped to it, the record of payments along with the annual tax receipts. It's all there. We could calculate, if we chose, the exact dimensions of our delusions. But we never do. We live here, after all.

Up and down the gentle curve of Beaver Place we see cedar-shake siding, colonial pillars, the jutting chins of split-levels, each of them bought in hours of panic, but with each one, some particular fantasy fulfilled. The house they never had as children perhaps. The house that will do for now, before the move to the big one on the river lot. The house where visions of dynasty are glimpsed, a house future generations will visit, spend holidays in and write up in memoirs. Why not?

Something curious. One day last week,

having been especially energetic about Susanna Moodie and turning out six pages in one morning, I found myself out of paper. There must be some in the house, I thought and, although I prefer soft, pulpy yellow stuff, anything is useable in a pinch, I searched Meredith's room first, being careful not to disturb her things. Everything there is so carefully arranged; she has all sorts of curios, souvenirs, snapshots, a music award stencilled on felt, animal figurines she collected as a very young child, cosmetics in a pearly pale shade standing at attention on her dresser. Everything but paper.

In Richard's room I found desk drawers filled with Anita Spalding's letters, each one taped shut from prying eyes. Mine perhaps? Safety patrol badges, a map of England with an inked star on Birmingham, a copy of *Playboy*, hockey pictures, but not a single sheet of useable paper.

Martin will have some, I thought. I went downstairs to the family room to look in his desk. Nothing in the top drawer except his Xeroxed paper on *Paradise Regained*, recently rejected by the *Milton Quarterly*. In his second drawer were clipped notes for an article on *Samson Agonistes* and offprints of an article he had had printed in *Renaissance Studies*, the one on Milton's childhood which he had researched in England. The third drawer was full of wool.

I blinked. Unbelievable. The drawer was stuffed to the top with brand new hanks of wool, still with their little circular bands around them. I reached in and touched them. Blue, red, yellow, green; fat four-ounce bundles in all colours. Eight of them. Lying on their sides in Martin's drawer. Wool.

It couldn't be for me. I hate knitting and detest crocheting. For Meredith perhaps? An early Christmas present? But she hadn't knitted anything since Brownies, six years ago, and had never expressed any interest in taking it up again.

Frieda? Frieda who comes to clean out the house on Wednesday? She knits, and it is just possible, I thought, that it was hers. Absurd though. She never goes in Martin's desk, for one thing. And what reason would she have to stash all this lunatic wool in his drawer anyway? Richard? Out of the question. What would he be doing with wool? It must be Martin's. For his mother, maybe; she loves knitting. He might have seen it on sale and bought it for her, although it seemed odd he hadn't mentioned it to me. I'll ask him tonight, I thought.

But that night Martin was at a meeting, and I was asleep when he came home. The next day I forgot. And the next. Whenever it pops into my mind, he isn't around. And when he is, something makes me stumble and hesitate as though I were afraid of the reply. I still haven't asked him, but this morning I looked in the drawer to see if it was still there. It was all in place, all eight bundles; nothing had been touched. I must ask Martin about it.

As Meredith grows up I look at her and think, who does she remind me of? A shaded gesture, a position struck, or something curious she might say will touch off a shock of recognition in me, but I can never think who it is she is like.

I flip through my relatives — like flashcards. My mother. No, no, no. My sister Charleen? No. Charleen, for all her sensitivity, has a core of detachment. Aunt Liddy? Sometimes I am quite sure it is my old aunt. But no. Auntie's fragility is neurotic, not natural like Meredith's. Who else?

She has changed in the last year, is romantic and realistic in violent turns. Now she is reading Furlong Eberhardt's new book about the prairies. While she reads, her hands grip the cover so hard that the bones of her hands stand up, whey-white. Her eyes float in a concerned sweep over the pages, her forehead puzzled. It's painful to watch her; she shouldn't invest so much of herself in anything as ephemeral as a book; it is criminal to care that much.

Like my family she is dark, but unlike us she has a delicious water-colour softness, and if she were braver she would be beautiful. She is as tall as I am but she has been spared the wide country shoulders; there are some blessings.

It is an irony, the sort I relish, that I who am a biographer and delight in sorting out personalities, can't even draw a circle around my own daughter's. Last night at the table, just as she was cutting into a baked potato, she raised her eyes, exceptionally sober even for her, and answered some trivial question Martin had asked her. The space between the movement of her hand and the upward angle of her eyes opened up, and I almost had it.

Then it slipped away.

Last night Martin and I went to a play. It was one of Shaw's early ones, written before he turned drama into social propaganda. The slimmest of drawingroom debacles, it was a zany sandwich of socialism and pie-in-the-eye, daft but with brisk touches of irreverence. And the heroes were real heroes, the way they should be, and the heroines were even better. The whole evening was a confection, a joy.

During the intermission we stood in the foyer chatting with Furlong Eberhardt and his mother, our delight in the play surfacing on our lips like crystals of sugar. Mrs. Eberhardt, as broad-breasted as one of the Shavian heroines, encircled us with her peculiar clove-flavoured embrace. A big woman, she is mauve to the bone; even her skin is faintly lilac, her face a benign fretwork of lines framed with waves of palest violet.

"Judith, you look a picture. How I wish I could wear those pantsuits."

"You look lovely as you are, Mother," Furlong said, and she did; if ever a woman deserved a son with a mother fixation, it was Mrs. Eberhardt.

Martin disappeared to get us drinks, and Furlong, by a bit of clever steering, turned our discussion to his new book, *Graven Images*.

"I know I can count on you, Judith, for a candid opinion. The critics, mind you, have been very helpful, and thus far, very kind." He paused.

For a son of the Saskatchewan soil, Furlong is remarkably courtly, and like all the courtly people I know, he inspires in me alleys of unknown coarseness. I want to slap his back, pump his hand, tell him to screw off. But I never do, never, for basically I am too fond of him and even grateful, thankful for his most dazzling talent which is not writing at all, but the ability he has

35

to make the people around him feel alive. There is an exhausted Byzantine quality about him which demands response, and even at that moment, standing in the theatre foyer in my too-tight pantsuit and my hair falling down around my rapidly ageing face, I was swept with vitality, almost drunk with the recognition that all things are possible. Beauty, fame, power; I have not been passed by after all.

But about *Graven Images*, I had to confess ignorance. "I've been locked up with Susanna for months," I explained. It sounded weak. It *was* weak. But I thought to add kindly, "Meredith is reading it right now. She was about halfway through when we left the house tonight."

At this he beamed. "Then it is to your charming daughter I shall have to speak." Visibly wounded that I hadn't got around to his book, he rallied quickly, drowning his private pain in a flood of diffusion. "Public reaction is really too general to be of any use, as you well know, Judith. It is one's friends one must rely upon." He pronounced the word friends with such a silky sound that, for an instant, I wished he were a different make of man.

"Meredith would love to discuss it with you, Furlong," I told him honestly. "Besides, she's a more sensitive reader of fiction than I am. You, of all people, know fiction isn't my thing."

"Ah yes, Judith," he said. "It's your old Scarborough puritanism, as I've frequently told you. Judith Gill, my girl, basically you believe fiction is wicked and timewasting. The devil's work. A web of lies."

"You just might be right, Furlong."

When Martin came back with our drinks, Furlong issued a general invitation to attend his publication party in November. He beamed at Martin, "You two must plan to come."

"Hmmm," Martin murmured noncommittally. He doesn't really like Furlong; the relationship between them, although they teach in the same department, is one of tolerant scorn.

The lights dipped, and we found our way back to our seats. Back to the lovely arched setting, lit in some magical way to suggest sunrise. Heroines moved across the broad stage like clipper ships, their throats swollen with purpose. The play wound down and so did they in their final speeches. Holy holy, the crash of applause that always brings tears stinging to my eyes.

All night long memories of the play boiled through my dreams, a plummy jam stewed from those intelligent, cruising, early-century bosoms. Hour after hour I rode on a sea of breasts: the exhausted mounds of Susanna Moodie, touched with lamplight. The orchid hills and valleys of Mrs. Eberhardt, bubbles of yeast. The tender curve of my daughter Meredith. The bratty twelve-year-old tits of Anita Spalding, rising, falling, melting, twisting in and out of the heavy folds of sleep.

I woke to find Martin's arm flung across my chest; the angle of his skin was perceived and recognized, a familiar coastline. The weight was a lever that cut off the electricity of dreams, pushing me down, down through the mattress, down through the floor, down, into the spongy cave of the blackest sleep. Oblivion.

October

The first frost this morning, a landmark. At breakfast Martin talks about snow tires and mentions a sale at Canadian Tire. After school these days Richard plays football with his friends in the shadowy yard, and when they thud to the grass, the ground rings with sound. Watching them, I am reassured.

It is almost dark now when we sit down to dinner. Meredith has found some candles in the cupboard, bent out of shape with the summer heat but still useable, so that now our dinners are washed with candlelight. I make pot roast which they love and mashed potatoes which make me think of Susanna Moodie. In the evening the children have their homework. Martin goes over papers at his desk or reads a book, sitting in the yellow chair, his feet resting on the coffeetable, and he hums. Richard and Meredith bicker lazily. Husband, children, they are not so much witnessed as perceived, flat leaves which grow absently from a stalk in my head, each fitting into the next, all their curving edges perfect. So far, so far. It seems they require someone, me, to watch them; otherwise they would float apart and disintegrate.

I watch them. They are as happy as can be expected. What is the matter with me, I wonder. Why am I always the one who watches?

One day this week I checked into the Civic Hospital for a minor operation, a delicate, feminine, unspeakable, minimal nothing, the sort of irksome repair work which I suppose I must expect now that I am forty.

A minor piece of surgery, but nevertheless requiring a general anaesthetic. Preparation, sleep, recovery, a whole day required, a day fully erased from my life. Martin drove me to the hospital at nine and came to take me home again in the evening. The snipping and sewing were entirely satisfactory, and except for an hour's discomfort, there were no after effects. None. I am in service again. A lost day, but there was one cheering interlude.

Shortly before the administering of the general anaesthetic, I was given a little white pill to make me drowsy. In a languorous trance I was then wheeled on a stretcher to a darkened room and lined up with about twelve other people, male and female, all in the same condition. White-faced nurses tiptoed between our parked rows, whispering. Far below us in another world, cars honked and squeaked.

Lying there semidrugged, I sensed a new identity: I was exactly like a biscuit set out to bake, just waiting my turn in the oven. I moved my head lazily to one side and found myself face to face, not six inches away from a man, another biscuit. His eyes met mine, and I watched him fascinated, a slow-motion film, as he laboured to open his mouth and pronounce with a slur, "Funny feeling, eh?"

"Yes," I said. "As though we were a tray of biscuits."

"That's right," he said crookedly.

Surprised, I asked, "What are you here for?"

"The old water works," he said yawning. "But nothing major."

Kidneys, bladder, urine; a diagram flashed in my brain. "That's good," I mumbled. Always polite. I cannot, even here, escape courtesy.

"What about you?" he mouthed, almost inaudible now.

"One of those female things," I whispered. "Also not major."

"You married?"

"Yes. Are you?" I asked, realizing too late that he had asked because of the nature of my complaint, not because we were comparing our status as we might had we met at a party.

"Yes," he said. "I'm married. But not happily."

"Pardon?" Courtesy again, the scented phrase. Our mother had always insisted we say pardon and, as Charleen says, we are children all our lives, obedient to echoes.

"Not happily," he said again. "Married yes," he made an effort to enunciate, "but not happily married."

A surreal testimony. It must be the anaesthetic, I thought, pulling an admission like that from a sheeted stranger. The effect of the pill or perhaps the rarity of the circumstances, the two of us lying here nose to nose, almost naked under our thin sheets, horizontal in midmorning, chemical-smelling limbo, our conversation somehow crisped into truth.

"Too bad," I said with just a shade of sympathy.

"You happily married?" he asked.

"Yes," I murmured, a little ashamed at the affirmative ring in my voice. "I'm one of the lucky ones. Not that I deserve it."

"What do you mean, not that you deserve it?"

"I don't know."

"Well, you said it," he said crossly.

"I just meant that I'm not all that terrific a wife. You know, not self-sacrificial." I groped for an example. "For instance, when

Martin asked me to type something for him last week. Just something short."

"Yeah?" His mouth made a circle on the white sheet.

"I said, what's the matter with Nell? That's his secretary."

"He's got a secretary, eh?"

"Yes," I admitted, again stung with guilt. This was beginning to sound like a man who didn't have a secretary. "She's skinny though," I explained. "A real stick. And he shares her with two other professors."

"I see. I see." His voice dropped off and I thought for a minute that he'd fallen asleep.

Pressing on anyway I repeated loudly, "So I said, what's the matter with Nell?"

"And what did he say to that?" the voice came.

"Martin? Well, he just said, 'Never mind, Judith.' But then I felt so mean that I went ahead and did it anyway."

"The typing you mean?"

"Uh huh."

"So you're not such a rotten wife," he accused me.

"In a way," I said. "I did it, but it doesn't count if you're not willing." Where had I got that? Girl Guides maybe.

"I never ask my wife to type for me."

"Why not?" I asked.

"Typing I don't need."

43

"Maybe you ask for something else," I suggested, aware that our conversation was slipping over into a new frontier.

"Just to let me alone, to let me goddamned alone. Every night she has to ask me what I did all day. At the plant. She wants to know, she says. I tell her, look, I lived through it once, do I have to live through it twice?"

"I see what you mean," I said, hardly able to remember what we were talking about.

"You do?" Far away in his nest of sheets he registered surprise.

"Yes. I know exactly what you mean. As my mother used to say, 'I don't want to chew my cabbage twice.' "

"You mean you don't ask your husband what he did all day?"

"Well," I said growing weary, "no I don't think I ever do. Poor Martin."

"Christ," he said as two nurses began rolling him to the doorway. "Christ. I wish I was married to you."

"Thank you," I called faintly. "Thank you, thank you."

Absurdly flattered, I too was wheeled away. Joy closed my eyes, and all I remember seeing after that was a blur of brilliant blue.

"You haven't read it yet, have you?" Meredith accuses me.

44

"Read what yet?" I am ironing in the kitchen, late on a Thursday afternoon. Pillowcases, Martin's shirts. I am travelling across the yokes, thinking these shirts I bought on sale are no good. Just a touch-up they're supposed to need, but the point of my iron is required on every seam.

"You haven't read Furlong's book?" Meredith says sharply.

"The new one you mean?"

"Graven Images."

"Well," I say apologetically, letting that little word "well" unwind slowly, making a wavy line out of it the way our mother used to do, "well, you know how busy I've been."

"You read Pearson's book."

"That was different."

Abruptly she lapses into confidence. "It's the best one he's written. You've just got to read it. That one scene where Verna dies. You'll love it. She's the sister. Unmarried. But beautiful, spiritual, even though she never had a chance to go to school. She's blind, but she has these fantastic visions. Honestly, when you stop to think that here you have a man, a man who is actually writing from inside, you know, from inside a woman's head. It's unbelievable. That kind of intuition."

"I'm planning to read it," I assure her earnestly, for I want to make her happy.

"But there's the Susanna thing, and when I'm not working on that, there's the ironing. One thing after another."

"You know that's not the reason you haven't read it," she says, her eyes going icy.

I put down the iron, setting it securely on its heel. "All right, Meredith. You tell me why."

"You think he's a dumb corny romantic. Flabby. Feminine."

"Paunchy," I help her out.

"You see," her voice rises.

"Predictable. That's it, if you really want to know, Meredith."

"I don't know how you can say that."

"Easy." I tell her. "This is his tenth novel, you know, and I've read them all. Every one. So I've a pretty good idea what's in this one. The formula, you might say, is familiar."

"What's it about then?" her voice pleads, and I don't dare look at her.

I shake a blouse vigorously out of the basket. "First there's the waving wheat. He opens, Chapter One, to waving wheat. Admit it, Meredith, Saskatchewan in powder form. Mix with honest rain water for native genre."

"He grew up there."

"I know, Meredith, I know. But he doesn't live there now, does he? He lives here in the east. For twenty years he's lived in the east. And he isn't a farmer. He's a writer. And when he's not being a writer, he's being a professor. Don't forget about that."

"Roots matter to some people," she says in a tone which accuses me of forgetting my own. Nurtured on the jointed avenues of Scarborough, did that count?

"All right," I say. "Then you move into his storm chapter. Rain, snow, hail, locusts maybe. It doesn't matter as long as it's devastating. Echoes of Moses. A punishing storm. To remind them they're reaching too high or sinning too low. A holocaust and, I grant you this, very well done. Furlong is exceptional on storms."

"This book really is different. There's another plot altogether."

I rip into a shirt of Richard's. "Then the characters. Three I can be sure of. The Presbyterian Grandmother. And sometimes Grandfather too, staring out from his little chimney corner, all-knowing, all-seeing, but, alas, unheeded. Right, Meredith?"

Stop, I tell myself. You're enjoying this. You're a cruel, cynical woman piercing the pink valentine heart of your own daughter, shut up, shut up.

She mumbles something I don't catch.

"Then," I say, "we're into the wife. She endures. There's nothing more to say about her except that she endures. But her husband, rampant with lust, keep your eye on him."

"You haven't even read it."

"Watch the husband, Meredith. Lust will undo him. Furlong will get him for sure with a horde of locusts. Or a limb frozen in the storm and requiring a tense kitchen-table amputation."

"Influenza," Meredith murmurs. "But the rest really is different."

"And we close with more waving wheat. Vibrations from the hearthside saying, if only you'd listened."

"It's not supposed to be real life. It's not biography," she says, giving that last word a nasty snap. "It's sort of a symbol of the country. You have to look at it as a kind of extended image. Like in Shakespeare."

"I'm going to read it," I tell her as I fold the ironing board, contrite now. "I might even settle down with it tonight."

We've had the book since August. Furlong brought me one, right off the press one steaming afternoon. Inscribed "To Martin and Judith Who Care." Beautiful thought, but I cringed reading it, hoping Martin wouldn't notice. Furlong seems unable to resist going the quarter-inch too far.

Furlong's picture on the back of the book is distressingly authority. One can see evidence of a tally taken, a check list fulfilled.

Beard and moustache, of course. White turtleneck exposed at the collar of an overcoat.
Tweed and cablestitch juxtaposed, a gen-
eration-straddling costume testifying to
eclectic respectability.

A pipe angles from the corner of his
mouth! Its bowl is missing, the outlines
lost in the dark shadow of the overcoat, so
that for a moment I thought it was a ciga-
rillo or maybe just a fountain pen he was
sucking on. But no, on close examination
I could see the shine of the bowl. Everything in place.

The picture is two-colour, white and a
sort of olive tone, bleeding off the edges,
Time-Life style. Behind him a microcosm
of Canada — a fretwork of bare branches
and a blur of olive snow, man against nature.

His eyes are mere slits. Snow glare? The
whole expression is nicely in place, a costly
membrane, bemused but kindly, academic
but gutsy. The photographer has clearly
demanded detachment.

The jacket blurb admits he teaches creative writing in a university, but couched
within this apology is the information that
he has also swept floors, reported news,
herded sheep, a man for all seasons, our
friend Furlong.

Those slit eyes stick with me as I put
away the ironing; shirts on hangers, hand-

49

kerchiefs in drawers, pillowcases in the cupboard. They burn twin candles in my brain, and their nonchalance fails to convince me; I feel the muscular twitch of effort, the attempt to hold, to brave it out.

Poor Furlong, christened, legend has it, by the first reviewer of his first book who judged him a furlong ahead of all other current novelists. Before that he was known as Red, but I know the guilty secret of his real name: it is Rudyard. His mother let it slip one night at a department sherry party, then covered herself with a flustered apology. We grappled, she and I, in a polite but clumsy exchange, confused and feverish, but I am not a biographer for nothing; I filed it away; I remember the name Rudyard. Rudyard. Rudyard. I think of it quite often, and in a way I love him, Rudyard Eberhardt. More than I could ever love Furlong.

Meredith slips past me on the stairs. She is on her way to her room and she doesn't speak; she doesn't even look at me. What have I done now?

"Martin."
"Yes."
"What are you doing?"
"Just going over some notes."
"Lecture notes?"
"Yes."

It is midnight, the children are sleeping, and we are in bed. Martin is leaning into the circle of light given off by our tiny and feeble bedside lamp, milkglass, a nobbly imitation with a scorched shade.

"Do you know I've never heard you give a lecture?"

"You hate Milton." He says this gently, absently.

"I know. I know. But I'd like to hear you anyway."

"You'd be bored stiff."

"Probably. But I'd like to see what your style is like."

"Style?"

"You know. Your lecturing style."

"What do you think it's like?" He doesn't raise his eyes from his pile of papers.

But I reply thoughtfully. "Orderly, I'm sure you're orderly. Not too theatrical, but here and there a flourish. An understated flourish though."

"Hummm."

"And I suppose you quote a few lines now and then. Sort of scatter them around."

"Milton is notoriously unquotable, you know." He looks up. I am in my yellow tulip nightgown, a birthday present from my sister Charleen.

I ask, "What do you mean he's unquotable. The greatest master of the English language unquotable?"

"Can you think of anything he ever said?"

"No. I can't. Not a thing. Not at this hour anyway."

"There you are."

"Wasn't there something like tripping the light fantastic?"

"Uh huh."

"It's hard to see why they bother teaching him then. If you can't even remember anything he wrote."

"Memorable phrases aren't everything."

"Maybe Milton should just be phased out."

"Could be." I have lost him again.

"Actually, Martin, I did hear you lecture once."

"You did? When was that?"

"Remember last year. No, the year before last, the year after England. When I was taking Furlong's course in creative writing."

"Oh yes." He is scribbling in the margin.

"Well, on my way to the seminar room one day I was walking past a blank door on the third floor of the Arts Building."

"Yes?"

"Through the door there was a sound coming. A familiar sound, all muffled through the wood. You know how thick those doors are. If it had been anyone else I wouldn't even have heard it."

"And it was me."

"It was you. And it's a funny thing, I couldn't hear a word you were saying. It was all too muffled. Just the rise and fall of your voice. And I suppose some sort of recognizable tonal quality. But it was mainly the rise and fall, the rise and fall. It was *your* voice, Martin. There wasn't a notice on the door saying it was you in there teaching Milton, but I was sure."

"You should have come in."

"I was on my way to Furlong's class. And besides I wouldn't have. I don't know why, but I never would have come in."

"I'd better just check these notes over once more."

"Actually, Martin, it was eerie. Your voice coming through the wood like that, rising and falling, rising and falling."

"My God, Judith, you make me sound like some kind of drone."

"It's something like handwriting." I propped myself up on one elbow. "Did you know that it's almost impossible to fake your handwriting? You can slant it backhand or straight up and down and put in endless curlicues, but the giveaway is the proportion of the tall letters to the size of the small ones. It's individual like fingerprints. Like your voice. The rhythm is personal, rising and falling. It was you."

"Christ, Judith, let me get this done so I can get some sleep."

"The funny thing is, Martin, that even when I was absolutely certain, I had the oddest sensation that I didn't know you at all. As though you were a stranger, someone I'd never met before."

"Really?" He reaches for my breasts under the yellow nylon.

"You were a stranger. Of course, I realized it was just the novelty of the viewpoint. Coming across you unexpectedly. In a different role, really. It was just seeing you from another perspective."

"Why don't we just make love?"

But I am still in a contemplative frame of mind. "Did you ever think of what that expression means? Making love?"

"They also serve who only stand and wait."

"Milton, eh?"

"Uh huh."

"Well, that's quotable."

"Fairly."

"Martin. Before you turn out the light, there's a question I've been wanting to ask you for weeks."

"Yes?"

"I don't want you to think I'm prying or anything."

"Who would ever suspect you of a thing like that?" His tone is only slightly mocking.

"But I notice things and sometimes I wonder."

His hand rests on the lamp switch. "Judith, just shoot."

"I was wondering, I was just wondering if you were really happy teaching Milton year after year?"

The light goes out, and we fall into our familiar private geometry, the friendly grazing of skin, the circling, circling. The walls tilt in; the darkness presses, but far away I am remembering two things. First, that Martin hasn't answered my question. And second — the question I have asked him — it wasn't the question I had meant to ask at all.

I spend one wet fall afternoon at the library researching Susanna Moodie, making notes, filling in the gaps.

This place is a scholarly retreat, high up overlooking the river, and the reading room is large and handsome. Even on a dark day it is fairly bright. There are rows of evenly spaced oak tables, and here and there groupings of leather armchairs where no one ever sits. The people around me are bent over enormous books, books so heavy that a library assistant delivers them on wheeled trolleys. They turn the pages slowly, and sometimes I see their heads bobbing in silent confirmation to the print. Unlike me, they have the appearance of serious scholars; distanced from their crisp stacks of notes, they are purposeful, industrious, admirable.

What I am doing is common, snoopy, vulgar; reading the junky old novelettes and serialized articles of Susanna Moodie; catlike I wait for her to lose her grip. And though she is careful, artfully careful, I am finding gold. The bridal bed she mentions in her story "The Miss Greens," a hint of sexuality, hurray. Her democratic posture slipping in a book review in the *Victoria Magazine*, get it down, get it down. Her fear of ugliness. And today I find something altogether unsavoury — the way in which she dwells on the mutilated body of a young pioneer mother who is killed by a panther. She skirts the dreadful sight, but she is really circling in, moving around and around it, horrified, but hoping for one more view. Yes, Susanna, it must be true, you are crazy, crazy.

Susanna Strickland Moodie 1803–1885. Gentle English upbringing, gracious country house, large and literary family, privately tutored at home, an early scribbler of stories. Later to emerge in a small way in London reform circles, a meeting with a Lieutenant Moodie in a friend's drawing-room, marriage, pregnancy, birth, emigration, all in rapid order. Then more children, poverty, struggle, writing, writing by lamplight, a rag dipped into lard for a wick, writing to pay off debts and buy flour. Then burying her husband and going senile, little wonder, at eighty, and death in Toronto.

It is a real life, a matter of record, sewn together like a leather glove with all the years joining, no worse than some and better than many. A private life, completed, deserving decent burial, deserving the sweet black eclipse, but I am setting out to exhume her, searching, prying into the small seams, counting stitches, adding, subtracting, keeping score, invading an area of existence where I've no real rights. I ask the squares of light that fall on the oak table, doesn't this woman deserve the seal of oblivion? It is, after all, what I would want.

But I keep poking away.

No wonder Richard seals his letter with Scotch tape. No wonder Meredith locks her diary, burns her mail, carries the telephone into her room when she talks. No wonder Martin is driven to subterfuge, not telling me that his latest paper has been turned down by the Renaissance Society. And concealing, for who knows what sinister purposes, his brilliant hanks of wool.

And John Spalding in Birmingham.

Poor John Spalding, how I added him up. Lecturer in English, possessor of a shrewish wife and precocious child, querulous and slightly affected, drinking too much at staff parties and forcing arguments about World Federalism, writing essays for obscure quarterlies; John Spalding, failed novelist, poor John Spalding.

How was he to know when he rented his flat to strangers that he would get me, Judith Gill, incorrigibly curious, for a tenant. Curious is kind; I am an invader, I am an enemy.

And he is a right chump, just handing it over like that, giving me several hundred square feet of new territory to explore. Drawers and cupboards to open. His books left candidly on the shelves where I could analyze the subtlety of his underlining or jeer at his marginal notations.

All that year I filtered him through the wallpaper, the kitchen utensils, the old snapshots, the shaving equipment, distilling him from the ratty blankets and the unpardonable home carpentry, the Marks-and-Spencer lamp shades and the paper bag in the bathroom cupboard where for mysterious reasons he saved burnt-out lightbulbs. Why, why?

The task of the biographer is to enlarge on available data.

The total image would never exist were it not for the careful daily accumulation of details. I had long since memorized the working axioms, the fleshy certitudes. Thus I peered into cupboards thinking, "Tell me what a man eats and I will tell you who he is." While examining the bookshelves, I recalled that, "A man's sensitivity is indexed in his library." While looking into the household accounts — "A man's bank balance betrays his character." Into his medicine cabinet — "A man's weakness is outlined by the medicines which enslave him."

And his sex life, his and Isabel's, strewn about the flat like a mouldering marriage map; ancient douche bag under a pile of sheets in the airing cupboard; *The Potent Male* in paperback between the bedsprings; a disintegrating diaphram, dusty with powder in a zippered case; rubber safes sealed in plastic and hastily stuffed behind a crusted Vaseline jar; half-squeezed tubes of vaginal jelly, sprays, circular discs emptied of birth control pills — didn't that woman ever throw anything away — stains on the mattress, brown-edged, stiff to the touch, ancient, untended.

Almost against the drift of my will I became an assimilator of details and, out of all the miscellaneous and unsorted debris in the Birmingham flat, John Spalding, wiry (or so I believe him to be), university lecturer, neurotic specialist in Thomas Hardy, a man who suffered insomnia and constipation, who fantasized on a love life beyond Isabel's loathsome douche bag, who was behind on his telephone bill — out of all this, John Spalding achieved, in my mind at least, something like solid dimensions.

Martin was busy that year. Daily he shut himself inside the walnut horizons of Trinity Library, having deluded himself into thinking he was happier in England than he had ever been before. The children were occupied in their daily battle with English schooling, and I was alone in the flat most of the time, restless between biographies, wandering from room to room, pondering on John and Isabel for want of something better to do.

Gradually they grew inside my head, a shifting composite leafing out like cauliflower, growing more and more elaborate, branching off like the filaments of a child's daydream. I could almost touch them through the walls. Almost.

Then I discovered, on the top shelf of John's bookcase, a row of loose-leaf notebooks.

His manuscripts.

I had noticed them before in their brown-and-buff covers, but the blank private spines had made me disinclined, until this particular day, to reach for them.

But taking them down at last, I knew before I had opened the first one that I was onto the real thing; the total disclosure which is what a biographer prays for, the swift fall of facts which requires no more laborious jigsaws. That first notebook weighed heavy in my hands; I knew it must all be there.

I had already known — someone must have told me — that John Spalding had written a number of novels, and that all of them had been rejected by publishers. And here they were, seven of them.

Since I had no way of recognizing their chronology, I simply started off in orderly fashion, with the notebook on the far left. In a week I had read the whole shelf, the work, I guessed, of several years. I swallowed them, digested them whole in the ivory-tinted afternoons to the tune of the ticking clock and the spit of the gas fire.

Before long a pattern emerged from all that print, the rickety frame upon which he hung his rambling stream-of-consciousness plots. Like ugly cousins they resembled each other. Their insights bled geometrically, one to the other.

The machinery consisted of a shy sensitive young man pitted against the incomprehensible world of irritable women, cruel children, sour beer, and leaking roofs. Suddenly this man is given the gift of perfect beauty, and the form of this gift varies slightly from novel to novel. In one case it appears in the shape of a poetry-reciting nymphet; in another case it occurs as a French orphan with large unforgettable eyes. And large unforgettable breasts. A friendship with a black man, struck up one day on a bus, which leads into a damp cave of brothels and spiritualism. Thus stimulated, the frail world of the sensitive young man swirls with sudden meaning, warming his heart, skin, brain, blood, bowels, each in turn. And then a blackout, a plunge as the music fades. The blood cools, and the hand of despair stretches forth. On the journey between wretchedness and joy and back to wretchedness, the young man is tormented by poverty and by the level of his uninformed taste. He is taunted by his mysterious resistance to the materialistic world or his adherence to fatal truths. Thousands and thousands of pages, yards and yards of ascent and descent, all totally and climactically boring.

Although, in fairness, the first book — at least the one on the far left which I judged to be first — had a plot of fairly breathless originality. I pondered a while over the significance of that. Had he lived this plot himself or simply dreamed it up? The rest of the books were so helplessly conventional that it was difficult for me to credit him with creativity at any level. Still, it seemed reasonable, since the least of us are visited occasionally by genius, that this book might have been his one good idea.

Later I was to ask myself what made me pry into another person's private manuscripts, and I liked to think that having discovered the bright break of originality in the first book, I read to the end in the hope of finding more. But it was more likely my unhealthy lust for the lives of other people. I was fascinated watching him play the role of tormented hero, and his wife Isabel too, floating in and out, bloody with temper, recognizable even as she changed from Janet, Ida, Anna, Bella, Anabel, Ada, Irene.

But more was to come. Besides the loose-leaf notebooks there was a slim scribbler which turned out to be a sort of writer's diary. I should have stopped with the novels, for opening and reading such a personal document made me cringe at his candour, my face going hot and cold as his ego stumbled beyond mere boyish postures, falling into what seemed like near madness. The passages were random and undated.

This constant rejection is finally taking its toll. I honestly believe I am the next Shakespeare, but without some sign of recognition, how can I carry on?

Constipation. It seems I am meant to suffer. An hour today in the bathroom

— the most painful so far. It is easy to blame I. Fried bread every morning. I am sick with grease. I am losing my grip.

Have not heard from publishers yet and it is now three months. No news is good news, I tell I. She smirks. Bitch, bitch, bitch.

My hopes are up at last. Surely they must be considering it — they've taken long enough over it. We are ready to go to London or even New York the minute we hear. Must speak to Prof B. about leave of absence. Should be no trouble as university can only profit by having novelist on staff.

Have been thinking about movie rights. Must speak to lawyer. Too expensive though. Could corner someone in the law faculty.

I am frightened at what comes out of my head. This long stream of negation. Life with I. and A. has become unreal. I exist somewhere else but where?

Manuscript returned today. Polite. But not very long note. Still, they must think I have some talent as they say they would like to see other manu-scripts. I expected more after six months. My first book was my best. A prophet in his own country. . . .

Stale, stale, stale. The year in Nicosia will do me good. Freshen the percep-tions. Thank God for Anita, who doesn't know how I suffer. Had another nosebleed last night.

I read the notebook to the end although the terrible open quality of its confessions brought me close to weeping. Silly, silly, silly little man. Paranoiac, inept, ridicu-lous. But he reached me through those disjointed bleeding notes as he hadn't in all his seven novels.

That shabby flat. I looked around at the border of brown lino and the imitation In-dian rug. Fluffy green chunks of it pulled away daily in the vacuum cleaner. Why did he save light bulbs? Did he believe, somewhere in his halo of fantasy, that they might miraculously pull themselves to-gether, suffer a spontaneous healing so that the filaments, reunited, their strength re-covered, were once again able to throw out light?

I put the notebook back on the shelf with the sad, unwanted novels. I never told any-one about them, not even Martin, and I never again so much as touched their tense covers. John Spalding and his terrible sorrowing stayed with me all winter, a painful bruising, crippling as the weather, pulling me down. I never really shook it off until I was back aboard the BOAC, strapped in with a dazzling lunch tray on my lap and the wide winking ocean beneath me.

November

Richard's friends are random and seasonal. There are the friends he swims with in the summer and the casual sweatered football friends. There is a nice boy named Gavin Lord whom we often take skiing with us but forget about between seasons. There is a gaggle of deep-voiced brothers who live next door. For Richard they are interchangeable; they come and go; he functions within their offhand comradeship. In their absence he is indifferent. And, of course, he has Anita.

Meredith's best friend is a girl named Gwendolyn Ackerman, an intelligent girl with a curiously dark face and a disposition sour as rhubarb. She is sensitive: hurts cling to her like tiny burrs, and she and Meredith rock back and forth between the rhythm of their misunderstandings; apology and forgiveness are their coinage. It is possible, I think, that they won't always be friends. They are only, it seems, temporarily linked together in their terrible and mutual inadequacy. After school, huddled in Meredith's bedroom, they minutely examine and torment each other with the nuances of their daily happenings, not only what they said and did, but what they nearly said and almost did. They interpret each other until their separate experiences hang in exhausted shreds. They wear each other out; it can't last.

For a quiet man, Martin has many friends. They exist, it seems to me, in separate chambers, and when he sees them he turns his whole self toward them as though each were a privileged satellite. A great many people seem to be extraordinarily attached to him. There are two babies in the world named after him. Old friends from Montreal telephone him and write him chatty letters at Christmas as though he really might care about their new jobs or the cottages they are building. His university friends often drop in on Saturday afternoons and, in addition, he hears regularly from his colleagues in England. He is not an effervescent man, but when he is with his friends he listens to them with a slow and almost innocent smile on his face.

His closest friend at the university is Roger Ramsay who teaches Canadian Literature. Roger has a fat man's face, round and red, with a hedge of fat yellow curls. But his body is long and lean and muscular. He is younger than we are, young enough so he is able to live with someone without marrying her, and he and Ruthie have an apartment at the top of an old Gothic house which is cheap and charming and only a little uncomfortable. Posters instead of wallpaper, ragouts in brown pots instead of roasts, candles instead of trilights, Lightfoot records instead of children. A growing collection of Eskimo carvings and rare Canadian books.

Ruthie St. Pierre is small, dark and brilliant; assistant to the head of the translation department in the Central Library. They both smoke the odd bit of pot or, as Roger puts it, they're into it. We love them, but what we can't understand is why they love us, but they do, especially Martin. In this friendship I am the extra; the clumsy big sister who is only accidentally included.

My closest friend is a woman named Nancy Krantz. She is about my age, mother to six children and wife to a lawyer named Paul Krantz, but that is strictly by the way. Nancy is not really attached to anyone, not even to me, I admit sadly. I am an incidental here as well.

She generally drops in unexpectedly between errands, usually in the morning. She almost always, but not quite, keeps the Volkswagen engine running in the driveway while we talk. She is in a rush and she dances back and forth in my kitchen with the car keys still jingling in her fingers. I cannot, in fact, imagine her voice without the accompaniment of ringing car keys. Our friendship is made up of these brief frenzied exchanges, but the quality of our conversation, for all its feverish outpouring, is genuine.

We talk fast, both of us, as though we accelerated each other, and there is a thrilling madness in our morning dialogues. Nancy has always just been somewhere or is on her way to somewhere — to an anti-abortionist meeting, to a consumers' committee, to a curriculum symposium. And into these concerns, which in the abstract interest me very little, she manages to sweep me away. I stand, coffee cup in one hand, wildly gesticulating with the other, suddenly stunningly vocal. The quality of our exchanges is such that she enables me to string together miles of impressive phrases; my extemporaneous self reawakened. I pour more coffee, and still standing we talk on until, with a loud shake of her key ring, Nancy glances at her watch and flies to the door. I am left steaming with exhaustion and happiness.

Today she has come from a committee which is fighting rate increases in the telephone service. It is her special quality to be able to observe these activities as though she were a spectator at a play. She can be wildly humorous. This morning, as a foot-note to her recital, she delivers what I think to be a stunning theory of life, for she has discovered the mechanism which monitors her existence.

Every month, she tells me, the water bill arrives in the mail. The Water and Sewerage Office informs her how much money she must pay and, in addition, how many gallons of water her household has consumed during the month. But that isn't all. Underneath that figure is another which is even more fascinating, the number of gallons which she and her family have consumed on the previous billing.

She has noticed something: since she and her husband Paul have been married, the number of gallons has gone up every month. There have been no exceptions over eighteen years, not one in eighteen years, twelve billings each year. By thousands and thousands of gallons she has gone steadily up the scale. It is inexorable. She and the meter are locked in combat. She would like to fool it once, to be very thrifty for a month, use her dishwater over again, make everyone conserve on baths, flush the toilet once a day, just to stop the rolling, rolling of the tide.

It has become a sign to her, a symbol of the gathering complexity of her life. Tearing open her water bill she finds her breath stuck in her chest. Travelling from gallon to gallon she is inching toward something. Is there such a thing as infinity gallons of water, she has wondered.

But recently it has occurred to her that she will never reach infinity. One month — the exact date already exists in the future, predestined — one month there will be a very slight decrease in number of gallons. And the next month there will be a further decrease. Very small, very gradual. It will work its way back, she says. And it will mean something important. Maybe that she is reverting to something simpler, less entangled.

She doesn't know whether it will be a good thing or bad, whether she is frightened or not of the day when the first decrease comes. But she sees her whole life gathered around that watershed. It may even mean the beginning of dying, she confides to the rhythm of her chromium-plated key ring.

Winter is about to fall in on us. Early this morning when I woke up I could almost feel the snow suspended over the backyard. Outside our window there was a dense gathering of white, a blank absence of sun, and through the walls of the house the blue air pinched and gnawed.

Downstairs in the kitchen I made coffee,

and I was about to wake Martin and the children when I heard a thin waterfall of sound coming from behind the birch slab door leading to the family room. I opened it and found the television on.

Richard and Meredith were sitting on the sofa watching. All I could see from the doorway were the backs of their heads, the two of them side by side, Richard leaning slightly forward, his hands on his knees. The sight of them, the roughed fur of their hair and the crush of pajama collars, and especially the utter attentiveness to the screen, made me weak for a moment with love.

"What's going on?" I asked hoarsely.

"Shhh," Richard rasped. "They're getting into the Royal Coach."

"Who?" I asked, and then remembered. It was Princess Anne's wedding day.

"How long have you two been up?" I asked.

"Five o'clock," Meredith said shortly, never for a moment taking her eyes off the picture. "Richard woke me up."

"Five o'clock!" I felt my mouth go soft with disbelief.

"It's direct by satellite," Richard said.

"But it will all be rebroadcast later," I said with sternness, feeling at the same time wondering amazement at their early rising.

"It's not the same though," Meredith said.

"They leave out half the junk," said Richard.

(Would Anita Spalding be watching too? In the Birmingham flat, linked through satellite with Richard? Probably.)

While the coffee breathed and burped in the kitchen, I sat on the arm of the sofa watching the glittering coach drive through London. A camera scanned the crowds, and the announcer reminded us how they had stood all night waiting. The London sky looked tea-toned, foreign, water-thin.

"I thought you didn't like Princess Anne," I challenged Meredith.

"I don't," she told me, "but this is a wedding."

Later, when Martin was up, we ate breakfast, and I told them about Princess Margaret's wedding. There was no satellite in those days, so we didn't have to get up at five o'clock to watch. Instead, a film of the wedding was shot in London and rushed into a waiting transatlantic jet.

We were at home in our first apartment; Martin was writing the final draft of his thesis. It was just after lunch, and Meredith, who was very young, had been put into her crib for a nap. Our television was old, a second-hand set with a permanent crimp in the picture.

The camera was focused on a bit of sky off the coast of Newfoundland and, while

Martin and I and millions of others stared at the blank patch, a commentator chattered on desperately about the history of royal weddings.

Finally a tiny speck appeared on the screen. The jet. We watched, breathless, as it landed. A man leaped out with an attaché case in his hand — the precious reels of film. Fresh from London. Rushed to the colonies. I remember my throat going tight. Stupid, but this man was a genuine courier, in a league with Roman runners and, though Martin and I were indifferent even then to royalty, we recognized a hero when we saw one.

We watched him race, satchel in hand, across the landing field and then into a flat terminal building where the projector was oiled and waiting. There was a moment's blackout, and the next thing we saw was the Royal Coach careening around Pall Mall. Miraculous.

While I was telling Meredith and Richard this story over cornflakes and toast, their eyes were fixed on me; they never miss a word. The genes are true; my children are like me in their lust after other people's stories.

Unlike Martin, whose family tree came well stocked with family tales, I am from a bleak non-storytelling family. I can remember my father, a tall, lank man who for forty years worked as inventory clerk in a screw factory, telling only one story, and this he told only two or three times. It was so extraordinary for him to tell a story at all that I remember the details perfectly.

A single incident fetched from his childhood: a girl in his high school tried to commit suicide by leaping into the stairwell. My father happened to be coming down a corridor just as she was sailing through the air. On impact she broke both her ankles and promptly fainted. This brought my father to the point of the story, the point as he conceived it being that the act of fainting was a benefice which spontaneously blocked out pain. He didn't explain to us why the girl was trying to take her life or whether she managed to live it afterwards. He seemed oddly incurious about such a dramatic event, and it must have been his bland acceptance of the facts which restrained us from asking him for details.

It is one of my fantasies that I meet this suicidal girl. She would be about seventy now — my father has been dead for ten years — and I imagine myself meeting her at a friend's. She is someone's aunt or family friend, and I recognize her the moment she touches on her attempted school suicide. I interrupt her and ask if she remembers a young boy, my father, who rushed to her when she fell and into whose arms she fainted. Yes, she would say, it happened just that way, and we would exchange long and meaningful looks, embrace each other, perhaps cry.

From my mother I can recall only two frail anecdotes, and the terrible thin poverty of their details may well account for my girlhood hunger for an expanded existence.

Once — I must have been about four at the time — my mother bought a teapot at Woolworth's, carried it home, and discovered when she opened it on the kitchen table that it was chipped. It was quite a nice brown teapot, she later explained to us, and it might have been bumped on the door coming out of Woolworth's. Or, on the other hand, it might have been chipped when she bought it. Should she return it?

She never slept a wink that night. After a week she had still not made up her mind what to do, and by this time she had broken out in a rash. It attacked the thin pink meat of her thighs and I can recall her, while dressing in the closet one morning, raising the hem of her housedress and showing me the mass of red welts. But I don't remember the teapot. She kept it for a year and used it to water her plants; then somehow it got broken.

Her other story, frequently told, concerned a friend of hers who greatly admired my mother's decorating talents. The friend, a Mrs. Christianson, had written to *Canadian Homes* suggesting they come to photograph our house for a future issue. For a year my mother waited to hear from the magazine, all the while keeping the house perfect, every chair leg free from dust, every corner cheerful with potted plants. No one ever called, and she came to the conclusion in the end that they were just too hoity-toity (a favourite expression of hers) to bother about Scarborough bungalows.

That was all we had: my father's adventure in the stairwell, which never developed beyond the scientific rationale for fainting, my mother's teapot and rash and her near-brush with fame. And a sort of half-story about something sinister that had happened to Aunt Liddy in Jamaica.

My sister Charleen, who is a poet, believes that we two sisters turned to literature out of simple malnutrition. Our own lives just weren't enough, she explains. We were underfed, undernourished; we were desperate. So we dug in. And here we are, all these years later, still digging.

On Tuesday Martin felt a cold coming on. He dosed himself with vitamin C and orange juice and went to bed early. He turned up the electric blanket full blast and shivered. His voice dried to a sandy rasp, but he never complained. It is one of the bargains we have.

Years ago, he claims, I put him under a curse by telling him that I loved him because he was so robust. Can I really have said such a thing? It seems impossible, but he swears it; he can even show me the particular park bench in Toronto where, in our courting days, I paid allegiance to his health. It has, he says, placed him under an obligation for the rest of his life. He is unable to enjoy poor health, he is permanently disbarred from hypochondria, he is obliged to be fit. So he went off to the university, his eyes set with fever and his pockets full of Kleenex.

I know the power of the casual curse. I have only to look at my children to see how they become the shapes we prepare for them. When Meredith was little, for instance, she, like any other child, collected stones, and for some reason we seized on it, calling her our little rock collector, our little geologist. Years later, nearly crowded out of her room by specimens, she confessed with convulsions of guilt that she wasn't interested in rocks any more. In fact, she never really liked them all that much. I saw in an instant that she had been trapped into a box, and I was only too happy to let her out; together we buried the rocks in the back yard. And forgot them.

Another example: Furlong, reviewing my first book for a newspaper, described me, Judith Gill, as a wry observer of human nature. Thus, for him I am always and ever wry. My wryness overcomes even me. I can feel it peeling off my tongue like very thick slices of imported salami, very special, the acidity measured on a meter somewhere in the back of my brain. Furlong has never once suspected that it was he who implanted this wryness in me, a tiny seedling which flourished on inception and which I am able to conceal from almost everyone else. For Furlong, though, I can be deeply, religiously, fanatically wry.

Just as for me Martin is strong and ruddy, quintessentially robust. But by the end of the week he was ready to give in. "Go to bed," I said. "Surrender."

Three days later he was still there, sipping tea, going from aspirin to aspirin.

I brought him the morning mail to cheer him up. "Just look at this," I said, handing him a milky-white square envelope.

I had already read it. It was an invitation to Furlong's lunch party in celebration of his new book. A one-thirty luncheon and a reading at three; an eccentric social arrangement, at least in our part of the world.

I squinted at the date over Martin's shoulder. "It's a Sunday, I think."

"It is," Martin said. "And I think —" his voice gathered in the raw bottom of his throat, "I think it's Grey Cup Day."

"That's impossible."

"I'm sure, Judith. Look at the calendar."

I counted on my fingers. "You're right."

He muttered something inaudible from the tumble of sheets.

"How could he do it?" I said.

"Well he did."

"He can't have done it on purpose. Do you think he just forgot when Grey Cup is?"

"Furlong's not your average football fan, you know."

"Nevertheless," I said, breathless with disbelief, "to give a literary party on Grey Cup."

"For 'one who embodies the national ethos,'" Martin was quoting from a review of *Graven Images*, "he is fairly casual about the folkways of his country."

"What'll we do?" I said. "What can I tell him."

"Just that we're terribly sorry, previous engagement, et cetera."

"But Martin, it's not just us. No one will come. Absolutely no one. Even Roger, worshipper though he be, wouldn't give up the game for Furlong. He'll be left high and dry. And there's his mother to consider."

"It's what they deserve. My God, of all days."

"And he's so vain he'll probably expect us to come anyway."

"Fat chance."

"I'd better phone him right away."

"The sooner the better."

"Right."

"And Judith."

"What?"

"Make it a firm no."

"Right," I said.

But I didn't have to phone Furlong. He phoned me himself late in the afternoon.

"Judith," he said, racing along. "I suppose you got our invitation today. From Mother and me."

"Yes, we did but —"

"Say no more. I understand. It seems I've made a colossal bloop."

"Grey Cup Day."

"Mother says the phone's been ringing all day. And I ran into Roger at the university. Poor lad, almost bent double with apology. Of course, the instant we realized, we decided on postponement."

"That really is the best thing," I said, relieved that I would not have to admit we put football before literature in this house.

"We'll make it December then, I think. Early December."

"Maybe you should check the bowl games," I suggested wanting to be helpful.

"Of course. Mother and I will put our heads together and come up with another date. Now I mustn't keep you from your work, Judith. How is it coming, by the way?"

"Well. I think I can honestly say it's going well."

"Good. Good. No more novel-writing aspirations?" he asked, and for an instant I thought I heard a jealous edge to his voice.

"No," I said. "You can consider me cured of that bug."

"That's what it is, a wretched virus. I can't tell you how I envy you your immunity."

"It was madness," I said. "Pure madness."

"That was Furlong on the phone," I told Martin when I took up his supper tray. Soup, toast, a piece of cheese. He was sitting up reading the paper and looking better.

"And? What did he have to say for himself?"

"All a mistake. He never thought of Grey Cup. So don't worry, Martin. It's been postponed. Way off in the future. Sometime in December."

"We might even be snowed in with luck," he said going back to his paper. "Anyway, that's the end of that story."

Story, he had called it. He was right, it was a story, a fragment of one anyway. A human error causing human outcry and subdued by a human retraction. A comedy miniaturized.

It's the arrangement of events which makes the stories. It's throwing away, compressing, underlining. Hindsight can give structure to anything, but you have to be able to see it. Breathing, waking and sleeping; our lives are steamed and shaped into stories. Knowing that is what keeps me from going insane, and though I don't like to admit it, sometimes it's the only thing.

Names are funny things, I tell Richard. We are having lunch one day, and he has asked me how I happened to name him Richard.

"I liked the 'r' sound," I tell him. "It's a sort of repetition of the 'r' in your father's name."

"And Meredith?" he asks. "Where did you get that?"

"I'm not sure," I tell him, for the naming of our babies is a blur to me. Each time I was caught unprepared; each time I felt a compulsion amidst the confusion of birth, to pin a label, any label, on fast before the prize disappeared.

Meredith. It is, of course, an echo of my own name, the same thistle brush of "th" at the end, just as Richard's name is a shadow of Martin's. Unconscious at the time; I have only noticed it since.

"I'm not sure," I tell Richard. "Names are funny things. They don't really mean anything until you enlist them."

Now he confides a rare fact about Anita Spalding, introducing her name with elaborate formality.

"You know Anita Spalding? In Birmingham?"

"Yes," I say, equally formal.

"Do you know what she does? She calls her parents by their first names."

"Really?"

"Like she calls her father John. That's his first name. And she calls her mother Isabel."

"Hmmmm." I am deliberately offhand, anxious to prolong this moment of confidence.

But he breaks off with, "But like you say, names are funny things."

"Richard," I say. "Do you know what Susanna Moodie called her husband?"

There is no need to explain who Susanna Moodie is. After all these months she is one of us, one of the family. Every day someone refers to her. She hovers over the house, a friendly ghost.

"What did she call her husband?" Richard asks.

"Moodie," I tell him.

"What's wrong with that? That was his name wasn't it?"

"His last name. Don't you get it, Richard? It would be like me calling Daddy, Gill. Would you like a cup of tea, Gill? Well, Gill, how's the old flu coming along? Hi ya, Gill."

"Yeah," Richard agrees. "That would be kind of strange."

"Strange is the word."

"Why'd she do it then? Why didn't she call him by his first name?"

"I don't know," I tell him. "It was the custom in certain levels of society in those days. And there's her sister, Catherine Parr Traill. She called her husband Mr. Traill. All his life. Imagine that. Moodie is almost casual when you think of Mr. Traill."

"I guess so," he says doubtfully.

"I like to think of it as a sort of nickname. Like Smitty or Jonesy. Maybe it was like that."

"Maybe," he says. "I suppose it depends on how she said it. Like the expression she used when she said it. Do you know what I mean?"

I did know what he meant, and it was a common problem in biography. Could anyone love a man she called by his surname?

Was such a thing possible? I would have to hear whether it was said coldly or with tenderness. One minute of eavesdropping and I could have travelled light-years in understanding her.

It was Leon Edel, who should know about the problems of biography if anyone does, who said that biography is the least exact of the sciences. So much of a man's life is lived inside his own head, that it is impossible to encompass a personality. There is never never enough material. Sometimes I read in the newspaper that some university or library has bought hundreds and hundreds of boxes of letters and papers connected with some famous deceased person, and I know every time that it's never going to be enough. It's hopeless, so why even try?

That was the question I found myself asking during the year we spent in England. My two biographies, although they had been somewhat successful, had left me dissatisfied. In the end, the personalities had eluded me. The expression in the voice, the concern in the eyes, the unspoken anxieties; none of these things could be gleaned from library research, no matter how patient and painstaking. Characters from the past, heroic as they may have been, lie coldly on the page. They are inert, having no details of person to make them fidget or scratch; they are toneless, simplified, stylized, myths distilled from letters; they are bloodless.

There is nothing to do but rely on available data, on diaries, bills, clippings, always something on paper. Even the rare photograph or drawing is single-dimensional and self-conscious.

And if one does enlarge on data, there is the danger of trespassing into that whorish field of biographical fiction, an arena already asplash with the purple blood of the queens of England or the lace-clutched tartish bosoms of French courtesans. Tasteless. Cheap. Tawdry.

That year in England I was restless. I started one or two research projects and abandoned them. I couldn't settle down. Everything was out of phase. My body seemed disproportionately large for the trim English landscape. I sensed that I alarmed people in shops by the wild nasal rock of my voice, and at parties I overheard myself suddenly raucous and bluff. It was better to fade back, hide out for a while. I became a full-time voyeur.

On trains I watched people, lusting to know their destinations, their middle names, their marital status and always and especially whether or not they were happy. I stared to see the titles of the books they were reading or the brand of cigarette they smoked. I strained to hear snatches of conversations and was occasionally rewarded, as when I actually heard an old gentleman alighting from his Rolls Royce saying to someone or other, "Oh yes, yes. I did know Lord MacDonald. We were contemporaries at Cambridge." And a pretty girl on a bus who turned to her friend and said, "So I said to him, all right, but you have to buy the birth control pills." And then, of course, I had the Spalding family artifacts around me twenty-four hours a day, and on that curious family trio I could speculate endlessly.

It occurred to me that famous people may be the real dullards of life. Perhaps shopgirls coming home from work on the buses are the breath and body of literature. Fiction just might be the answer to my restlessness.

"I think I might write a novel," I said to Martin on a grey Birmingham morning as he was about to leave for the library.

"What for?" he asked, genuinely surprised.

"I'm tired of being boxed in by facts all the time," I told him. "Fiction might be an out for me. And it might be entertaining too."

"You're too organized for full-time fantasy," he said, and later I remembered those words and gave him credit for prophecy. Martin is astute, although sometimes, as on this particular morning, he looks overly affable and half-daft.

"You sound like a real academic," I told him. "All footnotes and sources."

"I *know* you, Judith," he said smiling.

"Well, I'm going to start today," I told him. "I've been making a few notes, and today I'm going to sit down and see what I can do."

"Good luck," was all he said, which disappointed me, for he had been interested in my biographies and, in a subdued way, proud of my successes.

NOTES FOR NOVEL

Tweedy man on bus, no change, leaps off

beautiful girl at concert, husband observes her legs, keeps dropping program

children in park, sailboat, mother yells (warbles) "Damn you David. You're getting your knees dirty."

letter to editor about how to carry cello case in a mini-car. Reply from base player

West Indians queue for mail. Fat white

woman (rollers) cigarette in mouth says, "what they need is ticket home."

story in paper about woman who has baby and doesn't know she's preg. Husband comes home from work to find himself a father. Dramatize.

leader of labour party dies tragically, scramble for power. wife publishes memoirs.

hotel bath. each person rationed to one inch of hot water. Hilarious landlady.

Lord renounces title so he can run for House of Commons, boyhood dream and all that.

My random jottings made no sense to me at all. When I wrote them down I must have felt something; I must have thought there was yeast there, but whatever it was that had struck me at the time had faded away. There was no centre, no point to begin from.

I paced up and down in the flat thinking. A theme? A starting point? A central character or situation? I looked around the room and saw John Spalding's notebooks. That was the day I took them down and began to read them; my novel was abandoned.

After that I was too dispirited to do any writing at all. I spent the spring shopping and visiting art galleries and teashops and waiting for the end to come. I counted the days and it finally came. We packed our things, sold the Austin, gave the school uniforms away and, just as summer was getting big as a ball, we returned home.

Martin is better. Still on medication, but looking something like his real self. Today he went back to the university, and the house is quiet. For some reason I open his desk drawer, the one where the wool is.

It's gone. Nothing there but the wood slats of the drawer bottom and a paper clip or two. I look in the other drawers. Nothing.

I hadn't thought much about the wool while it was still there. I'd wondered about it, of course, but it was easy to forget, to push to the back of my thoughts. But now it has gone.

It has come and gone. I have been offered no explanations. Was it real, I wonder.

My hands feel cold and my heart pounds. I am afraid of something and don't know what it is.

December

The first snow has come, lush and feather-falling.

As a child I hated the snow, thinking it was both cruel and everlasting, but that was the hurting enemy snow of Scarborough that got down our necks, soaked through our mittens, fell into our boots and rubbed raw, red rings around our legs. It is one of the good surprises of life to find that snow can be so lovely.

Nancy Krantz and I skied all one day, and afterwards, driving home in her little Volkswagen with our skis forked gaily on its round back, we talked about childhood.

"The worst part for me," Nancy said, "was thinking all the time that I was crazy."

"You? Crazy?"

"It wasn't until I hit university that I heard the expression *déjà vu* for the first time. I had always thought I was the only being in the universe who had experienced anything as eerie as that. Imagine, discovering at twenty that it is a universal phenomenon, all spelled out and recognized. And normal. What a cheat! Why hadn't someone told me about it? Taken me aside and said, look, don't you ever feel all this has happened before?"

"Hadn't you ever mentioned it to anyone?"

"What? And have them know I was crazy. Never."

"You surprise me, Nancy," I said. "I would have thought you were very open as a child."

"Not on your life. I was a regular clam," she said, shifting gears at a hill. "And scared of my own shadow. Especially at night. At one point I actually thought my mother, my dear, gentle, plump, little mother with her fox furs and little felt hats was trying to put poison in my food. Imagine! Well, thank God for second-year psychology, even though it was ten years too late. Because that's normal too, a child's fear that his parents will murder him. And if they didn't, someone else would. Hitler maybe. Or some terrible maniac hiding out in my clothes cupboard. Or lying under my bed with a bayonet. Right through the mattress. Oh God. It was so terrible. And so real. I could almost feel the cold, steely tip coming through the sheet. But I never told anyone. Never."

"I wonder if children are that stoic today? Not to tell anyone their worst fears."

"Mine are pretty brave. I can't tell if they're bluffing or not, though. Weren't you ever afraid like that, Judith?"

"Of course," I said, "I was a real coward. But it's funny looking back. Do you know what it was that frightened me most about childhood?"

"What?"

"That it would never end."

"What do you mean?"

"I was frightened, but it wasn't so much the shadows in the cupboard that scared me. It was the terrible, terrible suffocating sameness of it all. It's true. I remember lying in bed trembling, but what I heard was the awful and relentless monotony. The furnace switching off and on in the basement. Amos and Andy. Or the kettle steaming in the kitchen. Even the sound of my parents turning the pages of the newspaper in the living room while we were supposed to be going to sleep. My mother's little cough, so genteel. The flush of the toilet through the wall before they went to bed. And other things. The way my mother always hung the pillowcases on the clothesline with the open end up, leaving just a little gap so the air could blow inside them. With a clothes peg in her mouth when she did it, always the same. It frightened me."

"I always thought there was something to be said for stability in childhood."

"I suppose there is," I agreed. "But I always hoped, or rather I think I actually knew, that there was another world out there and that someday I would walk away and live in it. But the long, long childhood nearly unhinged me. Take the floor tiles in our kitchen at home. I can tell you exactly the pattern of our floor in Scarborough, and it was a complicated pattern too. Blue squares with a yellow fleck, alternating in diagonal stairsteps with yellow squares with brown flecks. And I can tell you exactly the type of flowers on my bedspread when I was six and exactly what my dotted swiss curtains looked like when I was twelve. And the royal blue velvet tiebacks. It was so vivid, so present. That's what I was afraid of. All those details. And their claim on me."

"And when you finally did get away from it into the other life, Judith — was it all you thought it would be?" She was driving carefully, concentrating on the road which was getting slippery under the new snow.

I tried to shape an answer, a real answer, but I couldn't. "Oh, I don't know," I said with a hint of dismissal. "The trouble is that when you're a child you can sense something beyond the details. Or at least you hope there's something."

"And now?" she prompted me.

"And now," I said, "I hardly ever think about the kind of life I want to live."

"Why not?"

"I suppose I'm just too preoccupied with living it. Much less introspective. And one thing about writing biography is that you tend to focus less on your own life. But I think of Richard and Meredith sometimes, and wonder if they're taking it all in."

"The pattern on the kitchen floor?"

"Yes. All of it. And I wonder if they're waiting for it to be over."

"Maybe it's all a big gyp," Nancy said. "Maybe the whole thing is a big gyp the way Simone de Beauvoir says at the end of her autobiography. Life is a gyp."

I nodded. It was warm in the car and I felt agreeable and sleepy. My legs and back ached pleasantly, and I thought that the snow blowing across the highway looked lovely in the last of the afternoon light. The motor hummed and the windshield wipers made gay little grabs at the snow.

"It can't all be a gyp," I told her. "It's too big. It can't be."

And we left it at that.

"Judith." Martin called to me one evening after dinner. "Come quick. See who's being interviewed on television."

I dropped the saucepan I was scraping and peeled off my rubber gloves. Probably Eric Kierans, I thought. He is my favourite politician with his sluggish good sense so exquisitely smothered in rare and perfect modesty. Or it might be Malcolm Muggeridge who, nimble-tongued, year after year, poured out a black oil stream of delicious hauteur.

But it was neither; it was Furlong Eberhardt being interviewed about his new book.

I sank down on the sofa between Martin and Meredith and stared at Furlong. We were tuned to a local channel, and this was a relaxed and informal chat. The young woman who was interviewing him was elegantly low-key in a soft shirtdress and possessed of a chuckly throatiness such as I had always desired for myself.

"Mr. Eberhardt —" she began.

"My friends always call me by my first name," he beamed at her, but she scurried past him with her next question.

"Perhaps you could tell our viewers who haven't yet read *Graven Images* a little about how you came upon the idea for it."

Furlong leaned back, his face open with amusement, and spread his arms hopelessly. "You know," he said, "that's a perfectly impossible question to ask a writer. How and where he gets his ideas."

Smiling even harder than before, she refused to be put down. "Of course, I know every writer has his own private source of imagination, but *Graven Images*, of all your books, tells such an extraordinary story that we thought you might want to tell us a little about how the idea for the book came to you."

Furlong laughed. He drew back his head and laughed aloud, though not without kindness.

The interviewer waited patiently, leaning forward slightly, her hands in a hard knot.

"All I can tell you," he said, composing himself and assuming his academic posture, "is that a writer's sources are never simple. Always composite. The idea for *Graven Images* came to me in pieces. True, I may have had one generous burst of inspiration, for which I can only thank whichever deity it is who presides over creative imagination. But the rest came with less ease, torn daily out of the flesh as it were."

"I see," the interviewer said somewhat coldly, for plainly she felt he was toying with her. "But Mr. Eberhardt, this new novel seems to have an increased vigour. A new immediacy." She had recaptured her lead and was pinning him down.

Furlong turned directly into the camera and was caught in a flattering close-up, the model of furrowed thoughtfulness. "You may be right," he nodded in response. "You just may be right. But on the other hand, I wouldn't have thought I was exactly washed up as a writer before *Graven Images.*"

"If I may quote one of the critics, Mr. Eberhardt —"

"Furlong. Please," he pleaded.

"Furlong. One of the critics," she rattled through her notes, cleared her throat and read, "Eberhardt's new book is brisk and original, as fast moving and exciting as a movie."

"Ah," he said his hands pulling together beneath his beard. "You may be interested to know that it is soon to become a film."

Her eyes widened. "*Graven Images* is to be made into a film?"

"We have only just signed the contract," he said serenely, "this afternoon."

"Well, I must say, congratulations are in order, Mr. Eberhardt. I suppose this film will be made in Canada?"

"Ah. I regret to say it will not. The offer was made by an American company, and I am afraid I can't release any details at this time. I'm sure your viewers will understand."

Her eyes glittered as she leaned meaningfully into the camera. "Wouldn't you say, Mr. Eberhardt, that it is enormously ironical that you, a Canadian writer who has done so much to bring Canadian literature to the average reader, must turn to an American producer to have your novel filmed?"

He was rattled. "Look here, I didn't go

to them. They came. They approached me. And I can only say that of course I would have preferred a Canadian offer but —" an expression of helplessness transformed his face — "what can one do?"

"I'm sure we'll all look forward eagerly to it, Mr. Eberhardt. American or Canadian. And it has been a great pleasure to talk to you tonight."

The camera grazed his face one last time before the fadeout. "An even greater pleasure for me," he said with just a touch too much chivalry.

Meredith sitting beside me looked flushed and excited, and Martin was muttering with unaccustomed malice, "He's got it made now."

"What do you mean?"

"Your friend Furlong has just struck it rich."

I shrugged. "He's never been exactly wanting."

"Ah, Judith, you miss the point. A movie. This is no mere trickle of royalties. This is big rich."

"Well, maybe," I said, not really seeing the point.

"The old bugger," Martin said. "He's going to be really unbearable now."

"Tell me, Martin. Have you read it yet? *Graven Images*?"

"No," he said. "I keep putting it off."

"His party is next week. Sunday."

"I know. I know," he said despairingly.

"It may not be too bad."

"It'll be bad."

"Do you really despise him, Martin?"

"Despise him. God, no. It's just that he's such a perfect asshole. Worse than that, he's a phoney asshole."

"For example?" I asked smiling.

"Well, remember that sign he had in his office a few years ago? On his desk?"

"No. I never saw a sign."

"It was a framed motto. *You Shall Pass Through This Life but Once.*"

"Really? He had one of those? I can't imagine it. It seems so sort of Dale Carnegie for Furlong."

"He had it. I swear."

"And that's why he's an asshole?"

"No. Not that."

"Well, why then?"

"Because, after he got the Canadian Fiction Prize, and that big write-up in *Maclean's* and *The New York Times*, both in the same month —"

"Yes?"

"Well, right after that happened, he took down his sign. Just took it away one day. And it's never been seen since."

"He'd never own up to it now," I said.

"When I think of that sign and the way he stealthily disposed of it, another notch of sophistication — I don't know. That just seems to be Furlong Eberhardt in a nutshell. That one act, as far as I'm concerned, encapsulates his whole personality."

Meredith leapt from the sofa, startling us both. "I think you're both being horrible. Just horrible. So middle-class, so smug. Sitting here. It's character assassination, that's what. And you're enjoying it." She flew from the room with her breath coming out in jagged gasps.

For a moment Martin and I froze. Then he very slowly picked up the newspaper from the floor, reached for the sports page, and gave me a brief but hurting glance. "I don't understand her sometimes," was all he said.

It was then that I noticed Richard sitting quietly in a corner of the room, unobtrusive in his neat maroon sweater. He was watching us closely.

"What are you doing, Richard?" I asked.

"Nothing," he said.

Frantically, neurotically, harried and beleaguered, I am addressing Christmas cards. Richard, home with a cold, sits at the dining table with me; he is checking addresses, licking stamps, stacking envelopes in their individual white pillars; the overseas stack that will now have to be sent expensively by airmail, the unsealed ones with nothing but a rude "Judith and Martin Gill" scrawled inside them, the letters to old friends where I've crammed a year's outline into two or three inches — "A good year for us, Martin busy teaching, the children are getting ENORMOUS, am working on a new book, not much news, wish you were closer, happy holidays." And Martin's stack, the envelopes which Richard and I will leave unsealed so that tonight, after he gets home from the university, he can sit down and quickly, offhandedly write the funny, intense little messages he is so good at.

The afternoon wears on, and outside the window snow is falling and falling. Since noon we have had the overhead light on. Richard in striped pajamas looks pale.

This is a long, tedious task, and it irritates me to separate and put in order the constellations of our friends and to send them each these feeble scratched messages. But for the sake of the return, for the crash of creamy envelopes blazing with seals that will soon spill down upon us, I push on. For I want to hear from the O'Malleys who lived across the hall from us in our first apartment. I want to know if the Gorkys are still together and where the best man at our wedding, Kurt Weisman, has moved. Dr. Lawrence who supervised Martin's graduate work and his wife Bettina always

write us from Florida and so do the Gra-
hams, the Lords, the Reillys, the Jensens.
What matter that they were often dull and
that we might have drifted apart eventually? What matter that they were sometimes stingy or overly frank or forgetful?
They want to wish us a merry Christmas.
They want to wish us all the best in the
New Year. I can't help but take the printed
card literally; these are our friends; they
love us. We love them.

Richard is studying the airmail stamp
which goes on the letters to Britain. It is
a special issue with a portrait of the Queen,
an enormous stamp, the largest we have
ever seen. The image is handsome and the
background is filled in with pale gold. On
the corners of the tiny Rustcraft envelopes,
all I could find at this late date, it gleams
like a gem.

I write a brief note to the Spaldings, a
spray of ritual phrases. "We often remember the wonderful year we spent in Birmingham. The children have such happy
memories. Hope your family is well and
that you are having a mild winter, best
wishes from the Gills."

Richard seals it and affixes the great gold-
en stamp. "He's writing a book," he says.

"Who?" I ask absently.

"Mr. Spalding. He's writing a novel." Richard seldom mentions the Spaldings, but

when he does, it is abruptly, as though the words lay perpetually spring-loaded on the tip of his tongue.

"I suppose Anita wrote you about it?" I say inanely.

"Yes."

"And is it going well? The novel?"

"I don't know," he says. "But she says that sometimes he stays up all night typing."

"Well, I wish him luck," I say, thinking of his row of rejected manuscripts.

Richard makes no reply, and after a minute I ask him, "What's it about? The novel Anita's father is writing?"

"How should I know?" he says, suddenly querulous.

I snap back. "I only asked."

But I really would like to know what John Spalding is writing about. Maybe he's incorporating some new material from the year in Cyprus. Or perhaps reworking one of his old plots. He might even have resurrected his one good one.

I think of him typing through the night in the chilly, gas-smelling flat while the frowsy Isabel snores in a distant bedroom. I imagine his small frame, tense, gnatlike, concentrating on the impossible mass of a novel, and for a moment I see him as almost touchingly valiant.

Then guilt attacks me; a pain familiar

by now, a spurt of heat between my eyes, damn.

The Magic Rocking Horse was the name of the novel I wrote the year we came back from England. I intended, and for a while even believed, that the title would convey a subtle, layered irony — a childlike innocence underlying a theme of enormous worldliness.

But the novel never materialized on either level. Instead it simply stretched and strained along, scene after scene pitiably stitched together and collapsing in the end for want of flesh. For, unlike biography, where a profusion of material makes it possible and even necessary to be selective, novel writing requires a complex mesh of details which has to be spun out of simple air. No running to the public library for facts, no sleuthing through bibliographies, no borrowing from the neat manila folders at the Archives. That year the most obvious fact about fiction struck me afresh: it all had to be made up.

And where to begin? For two or three months I did nothing at all but think about how to begin. Dialogue or description? Or a cold plunge into action? Once or twice I actually produced a page or two, but later, reading over what I had written, I found the essential silliness of make-believe disturbing, and I began to wonder whether I really wanted to write a novel at all.

I discussed it with everyone I knew and got very little support. Roger and Ruthie told me, flatteringly, that it was a waste of my biographical skills. Nancy Krantz, sipping coffee, pursed her lips and pronounced, in a way which was not exactly condemning but almost, that she seldom read novels. Martin said little, but it was obvious that he viewed the whole project as somewhat dilettantish, and the children thought it might be a good idea if I wrote something along the line of Agatha Christie but transferred to a Canadian setting.

Furlong Eberhardt was the only one who volunteered a halfway friendly ear, and when he suggested one day that I might want to sit in on his creative writing seminar, it seemed like a good idea; a chance to sit down with a circle of other struggling fiction writers, sympathetic listeners upon whom I might test my material and who, in turn, might provide wanted stimulation or, as Furlong put it, might "prime the old pump."

Looking back, I believe the idea of again being a student appealed to me too. I bought a notebook and a clutch of yellow pencils, and each Wednesday afternoon I dressed carefully for the class which met in an airless little room at the top of the

Arts Building; my fawn slacks or my bronze corduroy skirt, a turtleneck, something youthful but never going too far, for what was the point of being grotesque for the sake of ten undergraduates ranging from eighteen-year-old Arleen whose black paintbrush hair fell to her hips, all the way to Ludwig, aged about twenty-four, horribly pimpled, who stared at me with hatred because I was married (and to a professor at that), because I lived in a house, because I was a friend of Furlong's, and possibly because my fingernails were clean.

No, I didn't fool myself that I was going to be one of them. And how could I since, despite my urging them to call me Judith, they always referred to me as Mrs. Gill. And when I read my short weekly contributions, always a quarter the length of theirs, they listened politely, even Ludwig, and never ventured any remarks except perhaps, very deferentially, that my sentences were a bit too structured or that my situations seemed a little, well, conventional and contrived.

Somewhat to my surprise I found that Furlong ran his creative writing seminar in a highly organized manner, beginning with what he called warming-up exercises. These were specific weekly assignments in which we were to describe such things as the experience of ecstasy or the effect of ennui, a dialogue between lovers one week and enemies the next.

I sweated through these assignments, typing out the minimum required words and, when my turn came, I read them aloud, feeling like a great overblown girl, red-faced and matronly, who should long since have abandoned such childish games.

The rest of them were not the least reticent; indeed they were positively eager to celebrate their hallucinations aloud. Arleen dragged us paragraph by paragraph through her thoughts on peace and mankind, and a girl named Lucy Rimer was anxious to split her psyche wide open, inviting us to inspect the tortured labyrinth of her awakening sexuality. Joseph, an African student, disgusted and thrilled us with portraits of his Ghanian grandparents. Someone called George Riorden dramatized his feeling on racial equality by having two characters, Whitey (a Negro) and Mr. Black (a white) dialogue over the back fence, reminding us, in case we missed it, of the express irony implied by their names. Ludwig poked with a blunt and dirty finger into the sores of his consciousness, not stopping at his subtle and individual response to orgasm and the nuances of his erect penis. On and on.

They were relentless, compulsive, unsparing, as though they had waited all their lives for these moments of catharsis, these Wednesday afternoon epiphanies. But looking around, when I dared to look around, I watched them wearing down, week by week exhausting themselves, and I wondered how long it could go on.

Eventually Furlong, who until then had merely listened and nodded, nodded and listened, called a halt and announced that it was time to begin the term project. Each of us was to write a short novel, about ten chapters he suggested, a chapter a week, which we were to bring to class to be read aloud and discussed. I breathed with relief. This was what I had hoped for, a general to command me into action and an audience who, by its response, might indicate whether I was going in the right direction.

I began at once on my first chapter, carefully introducing my main characters, providing a generous feeling of setting, and observing all the conventions as I understood them. It was all quite easy, and when my turn came to read, the class listened attentively, and even Furlong beamed approval.

And then I got stuck. Having described the personalities of my characters, detailed where they lived and what they did, I didn't know what to do with them next. The following week when my turn came, I apologized and said I was unprepared.

The others in the class seemed not to suffer from my peculiar malady which was the complete inability to manufacture situations, and I envied the ease with which they drifted off into fantasies, for although they strained my credulity, their inventiveness seemed endless.

A second week went by, leaving me still at the end of Chapter One. A third week. Furlong questioned me kindly after class.

"Are you losing interest, Judith?"

"I think I'm losing my mind," I said. "I just can't seem to get any ideas."

He was understanding, fatherly. "It'll come," he promised. "You'll see."

I waited but it didn't come, and I began to lie awake at night, frightened by the emptiness in my head. In the small hours of the morning, with Martin asleep beside me, I several times crept out of bed, padded downstairs, made tea, sat at the kitchen table and felt myself overcome by vacancy, barrenness, by failure.

A Wednesday afternoon came when I phoned Furlong before class pleading a violent toothache and a sudden dental appointment. The following Wednesday I went one step further: I absented myself without excuse. I was in descent now, set on a not-too-painful decline. There were days when I seldom thought about the novel at all.

I went skiing. I had my hair restyled at a place called Rico's of Rome and I shopped for new clothes. I painted the upstairs bathroom turquoise and joined a Keep Fit class. I went to the movies with Martin and Roger and Ruthie. I fringed and embroidered Richard's jeans, wrote a long letter to my sister Charleen. Everyone was kind; no one said a word about my novel. No one inquired about the seminar I was attending. No one except Furlong.

He kept phoning me. "You made a brilliant start, Judith. Your first chapter showed real strength. Head and shoulders above the rest of the little brats."

"But I can't seem to expand on that, Furlong. And not for want of trying."

"You say you really have been trying?"

"I have rings under my eyes," I lied.

"How about just letting your mind go free. Conduct a sort of private brainstorming. I sometimes find that helps."

"You mean you've felt like this too? Bereft? Not an idea in your head?"

"If you only knew. The truth is, Judith, I can be sympathetic because I haven't had a good idea in almost two years. And that, my old friend, is strictly entre-nous."

"And you've no solutions? No advice?"

"Try coming back to class. I know you think you can't face it at this point, but steel yourself. Most of what they write is garbage, but it's stimulation of a sort."

I promised, and I did actually go back for one or two sessions. And at home I forced myself to sit down and type out a paragraph every morning, but the effort was akin to suffering.

And then one day, just as Furlong had said, it came. In the middle of a dazzling winter morning, ten o'clock with the sun bold and fringed as a zinnia, it came. I would be able to save myself after all.

I would simply borrow the plot from John Spalding's first abandoned and unpublished novel, the one I had so secretly consumed in Birmingham. Such a simple idea. What did it matter that his writing was banal, boyish, embarrassingly sincere; the plot had been not only clever — it had been astonishingly original. Otherwise I wouldn't have remembered it, for like many rapid readers, I forget what I read the minute I close the covers. But John Spalding's plot line, even after all these months, was surprisingly vivid.

What I couldn't understand was why I hadn't thought of it before now. It was so available; what a waste to leave it stuck in a buff folder on a dusty shelf in an obscure flat in Birmingham, England. A good idea should never be orphaned. Luxuriously, I allowed the details to circulate through my veins, marvelling that the solution to my dilemma had been so obvious, so right, so free for the taking; it had an aura of inevitability about it which made me wonder if it hadn't been incubating in my blood all these months — germination, growth, now the burst of blossom.

I thought of the Renaissance painters, and happily, gleefully, drew parallels; the master painter often doing nothing but tracing in the lines, while his worthy but less gifted artisans filled in the colours. It had been a less arrogant age in which creativity had been shared; surely that was an ennobling precedent. For I didn't intend anything as crude as stealing John Spalding's plot outright. I already had my line-up of characters. My setting had been composed. All I needed to borrow was the underlying plot structure.

I woke the next day feeling spare, nimble, energetic, sinewy with health and muscle, confident, even omnipotent. I felt as though the blood had been drained out of me and replaced with cool-flowing Freon gas. My fingers were lively little machines exciting the keys; my eyes rotated mechanically, left to right, left to right; the carriage rocked with purpose. My brain ticked along, cleanly, accurately, uncluttered. The first day I wrote fifty pages.

I telephoned Furlong, shrilling, "I've finally got started."

"All you needed was an idea," he said. "Didn't I tell you."

The second day I wrote thirty pages. Somewhere I had lost my miraculous clarity; my idea had softened, lost shape; everything was blurring.

The third day I wrote ten pages and, for the first time, sat down to read what I had written.

Appalling, unbelievable, dull, dull. The bones of my stolen plot stuck out everywhere like great evil-gleaming knobs, accusing me, charging me. The action, such as it was, jerked along on dotted lines; there was no tissue to it. It was thin; worse than thin, it was skinny, a starved child.

Always when I had heard of writers destroying their manuscripts or painters shredding their canvases, I had considered it inexcusably theatrical, but now I could understand the desire to obliterate something that was shameful, infantile, degrading.

But I didn't tear it up. Not me, not Judith Gill, not my mother's daughter. I wrote a quick concluding chapter and retyped the whole thing before another Wednesday afternoon passed. I even made a special trip to Coles to buy a sky-blue binder with a special, newly patented steely jaw. And I carried it on the bus with me and delivered it to Furlong's office.

"But I don't want to read it to the class," I told him firmly. "Just do me a favour and read it yourself. And let me know what you think."

He nodded gravely. He consoled me with his tender smile. He understood. He would take it home with him. I got on the bus and came home and started cooking pork chops for our dinner. And it was then, with hot fat spattering from the pan and the pale meat turning brown that I lurched into truth.

Six-thirty; the hour held me like a hand. Doors slamming, water running, steam rising, the floor tiles under my feet squared off with reality. The clatter of cutlery, a knife pulling down on a wooden board, an onion halved showing rings of pearl; their distinct and separate clarity thrilled me. This was real.

I flew to the phone. My fingers caught in the dial so that twice I made a mistake. *Please be home, please be home!*

He was.

"Furlong. Listen, this is Judith."

"What on earth's the matter?"

"My novel. *The Magic Rocking Horse.*"

"But Judith, I just got home. I've hardly had more than a few minutes to glance at it. But tonight —"

"The point is, Furlong, I've decided not to go ahead with the novel."

"What do you mean — not go ahead? Judith, my girl, you've already done it."

"I mean I want you to dispose of it. Burn it. Tear it up. Now. Immediately."

"You can't be serious. Not after all your work."

"I can. I am." *Christ, he's going to be difficult.*

"Judith, won't you sleep on it. Give it some thought."

"I really mean this, Furlong. Listen to me. I mean it. I'm a grown-up woman and I know what I'm doing."

"Judith."

"Please, Furlong." I was close to tears. "Please."

He agreed.

"But on one condition. That you at least let me finish reading it. You may not have any faith in it, but I think, from the little of it I've seen, that it's not entirely hopeless."

"I don't care, Furlong, just as long as you keep your promise to get rid of it. And please don't ever discuss it with me. I couldn't bear that."

"Oh, all right. I promise, of course. But what are you going to do, Judith? Try another novel? Take another tack?"

"I'm going to write a biography."

"Who this time?"

"I was thinking of Susanna Moodie."

I had said it almost without thinking, only wanting to reassure Furlong that I wasn't mad. But the moment I uttered the name Susanna Moodie, I knew I was on my way back to sanity, to balance. I was on the way back to being happy.

The very next morning I began.

Sunday afternoon.

We are late, but since it is icy and since Martin is reluctant to go at all, we drive very slowly down the city streets to Furlong's party. I feel under my heavy coat for my wrist watch. We should have been there at one-thirty, and it's almost two now.

I am sitting in the front seat beside Martin, and through my long apricot crepe skirt the vinyl seat covers feel shockingly cold. Because of the snow I have had to wear heavy boots, but my silver sandals are in a zippered bag on the seat.

Meredith is in the back seat and she is leaning forward anxiously, concerned about being late and concerned even more about how she looks. She has been invited at the last minute. Mrs. Eberhardt phoned only this morning to suggest that she come along with us. I had hung about near the telephone listening, knowing for certain that she was being invited to replace some guest who was not able to come, knowing she would be filling in as a fourth at one of the inevitable little tables set up in Furlong's dining room. I had been to Furlong's parties before and knew how carefully the glasses of Beaujolais were counted out, how the seating would have been arranged weeks before and how the petit fours, the exact number, would be waiting in their boxes in the pantry. I would have cheered if Meredith had refused, if she had said she had other plans for this afternoon, but of course she didn't, nor would I have done so in her place.

Under her navy school coat she is wearing a dress of brilliant patchwork, made for her by Martin's mother last Christmas and worn only half a dozen times. She has done something marvellous and unexpected with her hair, lifted it up in the back with a tiny piece of chain, her old charm bracelet perhaps, and her neck rises slenderly, almost elegantly, out of the folds of her coat collar. But her nervousness is extreme.

Martin brakes for a red light and comes slowly, creepingly to a halt. I see his jaw firm, a rib of muscle, he wants only for this afternoon to be ended, to be put behind him.

Now is the moment, I think. Right now in the middle of the city, with apartment buildings all around us. I should ask him now about the eight bundles of wool that had been in his drawer. The fact that Meredith is here with us will only make it seem more normal, just a matter-of-fact question between husband and wife.

"Godamn," he mutters. "We should have bought those snow tires when they were on sale."

I sit tight and don't say a word.

Furlong and his mother live in a handsome 1930s building built of beef-red brick encircling a formal, evergreened courtyard. There is a speaking tube in the walnut foyer, rows of brass mail boxes; and today the inner door is slightly ajar, propped open with a spray of Christmas greenery in a pretty Chinese jardinière. We make our way up a flight of carpeted stairs to the panelled door with the brass parrot-headed knocker. Beyond it we can hear a soft rolling ocean of voices. Meredith and I bend together as though at a signal and exchange our boots for shoes, balancing awkwardly on each foot in turn. Only when we are standing in our fragile sandals does Martin lift the knocker.

It seems miraculous in all that noise that we can be heard, but in a moment Furlong throws open the door and stands before us. He is flushed and excited, and only scolds us briefly for being late. "Of course the roads are deplorable. Meredith, we are delighted, both of us, that you were able to come. You must excuse our phoning you so late, but it just occurred to us that you were a grown-up now and why on earth hadn't we asked you earlier. But give me your coats. I want you to taste my Christmas punch. Martin, you are a man of discernment. Come and see if you can guess what I've concocted this year."

He leads us into a softly lit living room where small circles of women in fluid Christmas dresses, and men, darkly suited and civilized, stand on the dusty-rose carpet. It is a large pale room, faintly period with its satin-covered sofa, its brocaded matching chairs, a cherry secretary, a Chinese table laid out with a punch bowl and a circle of cut-glass cups.

Furlong pours us ruby-pink cups of punch and watches, delighted, as we sip. "Well?" he asks Martin.

"Cranberry juice," Martin says.

"And vodka," I add.

"And something spicy," Martin continues. "Ginger?"

"Eureka!" Furlong says. "You two are the only ones who guessed. Meredith, I'm sure your parents will allow me to give you a little."

"Of course," she and I murmur together.

In a moment Mrs. Eberhardt is upon us, gracious and dramatic in deep purple velvet gathered between her breasts. "We were so afraid you had had an accident. This wretched snow. But I told Furlong not to worry. I knew you wouldn't let us down. Judith, you look delightful." She kisses my cheek. "I can't tell you how grateful we are that you let us have Meredith this afternoon."

Across the room Roger salutes us gaily. I am beginning to make out distinct faces in the early-afternoon light. I recognize Valerie Hyde who writes a quirky bitter-sweet saga of motherhood for a syndicated column in which she describes the hilarity of babyshit on the walls and the riotous time the cat got into the bouillabaisse just before the guests arrived. Her estranged husband Alfred is on the other side of the room with a hard-faced blonde in a sea-green tube of silk. Ruthie in cherry-coloured pants and a silk shirt is standing alone sipping cranberry-vodka punch and looking drunk and not very happy. I am about to speak to her when I see an immense fat man in a coarse, hand-woven suit. "Who's that?" I ask Mrs. Eberhardt.

She whispers enormously, "That's Hans Kroeger."

"The movie producer?"

"Yes," she says, hugging herself. "Wasn't it lovely he could be here. Furlong is so pleased."

Somewhere a tiny bell is ringing. I look up to see Furlong, silver bell in hand, calling the room to silence. "I know you must be ready for something to eat," he announces with engaging simplicity. "Lunch is ready in the dining room as soon as you are."

It is a large room painted a dull French grey. Half a dozen little tables are draped to the floor in shirred green taffeta — in the centre of each a basket of tiny white flowers.

Close behind me I hear Martin sighing heavily, "Jesus."

"Shut up," I say happily in his ear.

On the buffet table is Sunday lunch. There is a large fresh salmon trimmed with lemon slices and watercress, a pink and beautiful roast of beef being carved by a white-suited man from the caterers; cut-glass bowls of salad, tiny raw vegetables carved into intricate shapes, buttered rolls, crusty to the touch, fine and soft and patrician within; Mrs. Eberhardt's homemade mayonnaise in a silver shell-shaped dish, cheeses, fruit, stacks of Spode luncheon plates.

We serve ourselves and look about for our name cards on the little tables. I am by the window. There is heavy silver cutlery from Mrs. Eberhardt's side of the family, and a thick, luxurious linen napkin at each place. Furlong circulates between tables with red wine, filling each crystal glass a precise two-thirds full.

Everyone is talking. The room is filled with people eating and talking. Talk drifts from table to table, accumulating, rising, until it reaches the ceiling.

Roger is saying: "Of course Canadian culture has to be protected. For God's sake, you're dealing with a sensitive plant, almost a nursery plant. And don't tell me I'm being chauvinistic. I had a year at Harvard, remember. I tell you that if we don't give grants to our writers now and if we don't favour our own publishers now, we're lost, man, we're just lost."

Valerie Hyde is saying: "Of course women have come a long way, but don't think for a minute that one or two women in Parliament are going to change a damn thing. Sex is built-in like bones and teeth, and, remember this, Barney, there's more to sex than cold semen running down your leg."

Alfred Hyde is saying: "Tuesday night we had tickets to *The Messiah*. The tenor was excellent, the baritone was passable, but the contralto was questionable. The staging was commendable, but I seriously question the lighting technique."

Ruthie is saying: "There's just no stability to anything. Did you stop to think of just where this salmon comes from? The fisherman who caught this fish is probably sitting down to pork and beans right now. And what happens when all the salmon is gone? And that just might be tomorrow. What do you say to that? There's just no stability."

Hans Kroeger is saying: "Twenty per cent return on the investment. And that ain't hay. So don't give me any shit about bonds."

A woman across the room is saying: "Take Bath Abbey for Instance. Have you been to Bath Abbey? No? Well, take any abbey."

Furlong is saying: "In my day we talked about making a contribution. To the country. But that sounds facile, doing something for one's country. Now don't you agree that one's first concern must be to know oneself? Isn't that what counts?"

Meredith says: "I don't know. I really don't. Like in *Graven Images*, first things come first. I've started in on it for the third time. Empathy. That's what it all comes down to. I mean, doesn't it? Maybe you're right, but making a contribution still counts. I mean, really, in the end, doesn't it? Fulfillment, well, fulfillment is sort of selfish if you know what I mean. I don't know."

The blonde in green is saying, "Anyone from that socioeconomic background just never dreams of picking up a book. What

I'm saying is this, intelligence is shaped in preadolescence. Not the scope of intelligence. Anyone can expand, but the direction. The direction is predetermined."

A man is saying in a very low voice, "Okay, okay, you've had enough booze. Lay off."

Barney Beck is saying: "Class. You're damned right I believe in class. Not because it's good, hell no, but because it's there. Just, for instance, take the way kids cool off in the summer. You've got the little proletarians splashing in the street hydrant, right? And your middle-class brats running through the lawn sprinkler. Because lawns mean middle class, right? Then your nouveaus. The plastic-lined swimming pool. Cabanas, filter systems, et cetera. Then the aristocrats. You don't see them, not actually, because they're at the shore. Wherever the hell the shore is."

Mrs. Eberhardt is saying: "The important thing is to use real lemon and to add the oil one drop at a time, one drop at a time."

And I, Judith Gill, am spinning: I feel my animal spirit unwind, my party self, that progressive personality that goes from social queries about theatre series to compulsive anecdote swapping. I press for equal time. *Stop,* I tell myself. *Let this topic pass without pulling out your hospital story, your vitamin B complex story, your tennis story, your Lester Pearson snippet. Adjust your eyes. Be tranquil. Stop.* I admonish myself but it's useless. I feel my next story gathering in my throat, the words pulling together, waiting their chance. Here it is. I'm ready to leap in. "Speaking of bananas," I say, and I'm off.

Martin, at the next table, is not talking. What is he doing? He is lifting a forkful of roast beef and slowly, slowly, he is chewing it. What is he doing now?

He is listening.

January

It was on the first day of the new year that I discovered the reason for Martin's secret cache of wool; the explanation was delivered so offhandedly and with such an aura of innocence that I furiously cursed my suspicions. What on earth had I expected — that Martin had slipped over the edge into lunacy? That, saddened and trapped at forty-one, he might be having a breakdown? Did I think he nursed a secret vice: knitting instead of tippling? Or perhaps that he had acquired a mistress, a great luscious handicraft addict whose fetish it was to crochet while she was being made love to? Crazy, crazy. I was the one who was crazy.

On New Year's Day Martin sat talking to his mother and father who had come from Montreal for the weekend. His father is a professor too, himself the son of a professor; he teaches history at McGill. Gill of McGill, he likes to introduce himself to strangers. He is a spare, speckled man, happiest wearing the loose oatmeal cardigans his wife knits for him and soft old jackets, frayed at the pockets and elbows.

His habitual stance is kindly (a Franciscan kindness) and speculative; he is what is known in the world as a good man, possessing all the qualities of a Christian with the exception of faith.

The relationship between Martin and his father is such as might exist between exceedingly fond colleagues. Like brothers they flank Martin's mother, Lala to us, a small woman who except for an unmanageable nest of sparrow-brown, Gibson-girlish hair is attractive and bright, known to her friends in Montreal as a Doer. Her private and particular species of femininity demands gruff male attendance, and she is sitting now in our family room between "her two men," although that is a phrase which she herself would consider too cloying to use.

We have had a late breakfast, coffee and an almond ring brought by Lala from her local ethnic bakery in Montreal. The sun is pouring in through the streaky windows making us all feel drowsy and dull. Richard and Meredith, both of them blotchy with sleep, sprawl in front of the television watching the Rose Bowl Parade. There are newspapers everywhere, on the floor and on the chairs, thick holiday editions. And cups and saucers litter the coffee table. Lala leans back on the sofa, lazily puffing a duMaurier.

Grandpa Gill asks Martin how his course load is going and whether he is doing a paper at the moment. Lala leans birdlike toward them, eager to hear what Martin has to say. I too am roused from torpor. We all wait.

Martin tells his father about the paper that has been turned down. "I'll show it to you if you like," he says. "Apparently it just didn't measure up in terms of originality. One of the referees, anonymous of course, penciled 'derivative' all over it."

"That was bad luck," Grandpa Gill nods.

"What a shame, Martin," Lala adds.

I marvel for the thousandth time at the constancy and perfect accord with which they underscore their son's ability.

"To be honest," Martin continues, "it was pretty dull. But I'm working on something else now which might be a little different."

"Yes?" his mother sings through her smoke.

"Well," Martin says, addressing his father automatically, "I think I can say that I actually got this idea from you."

"Really?" Grandpa Gill smiles.

"Remember that chart you showed me. In your office last fall? A coloured diagram with the structure of world power charted in different colours?"

"Oh, yes. Of course. The Reynolds Diagram. Very useful."

"Well, after I saw that I got to thinking that it might be a good idea to use a diagram approach to themes in epic poetry. To *Paradise Lost* specifically."

"But how would you go about it?" his mother presses him.

"I thought it might be possible to make a graphic of it," Martin says. "Like the Reynolds Diagram, only using wool instead of paint since the themes are so mixed. In places it's necessary to interweave the colours. Sometimes, as you can appreciate, there are as many as four or five themes woven together."

His father nods and asks, "And how have you gone about it?"

"I thought about it for a long time," Martin says.

Where was I while he thought so long and hard?

"Finally I decided on a large rectangle of loose burlap for each of the twelve books. That way the final presentation could be hung together. For comparison purposes."

"I don't get it, Martin," I say, speaking for the first time.

He looks faintly exasperated. "All I did was to take a colour for each theme. For instance, red for God's omnipotence, blue for man's disobedience, green for arrogance, and, let's see, yellow for pride and so on. But you can see," he says, turning again to his father, "that one theme will predominate for a time. And then subside and merge into one of the others."

"And how do you know just where in the text you are?" Grandpa Gill asks.

"I wondered about that," Martin says.

Where was I, his wife, when he wondered about that?

"And I decided to mark off the lines along the side. I've got them printed in heavy ink. The secretary helped ink them in."

She did, did she?

"I think that sounds most innovative," his mother says nodding vigorously and butting out her cigarette.

"Is it nearly finished?" his father asks.

"Almost. I hope to present it in March."

"Present it where?" I ask, trying to control the quaver in my voice.

"The Renaissance Society. It's meeting in Toronto this year. I've already sent in an abstract."

"I'm anxious to see it," Lala says. "Is it here at home?"

"No. I've been putting it together at the university. But next time you come down I'll show it off to you. It should be all done by then."

"But Martin," I say, "you've never mentioned any of this to me."

"Didn't I?" He gazes at me. "I thought I did."

I give him a very long and level look before replying, "You never said a single word about it to me."

"Well, now that I have told you, what do you think?"

"Do you really want to know?"

All three of them turn to me in alarm. "Of course," Martin says.

Wildly I reach out for the right word — "I think it's, well, I think it's absurd."

"Why?" Martin asks.

"Yes, why, Judith?" his father asks.

I am confused. And unwilling to hurt Martin and certainly not wanting to upset his parents whom I like. But the project seems to me to be spun out of lunacy.

I try to explain. "Look," I say, "I can't exactly put it into words, but it sounds a bit desperate. Do you know what I mean?"

"No," Martin says, more shortly than usual.

"What I mean is, literature is literature. Poetry is poetry. It's made out of words. You don't work poems in wool."

"What you're saying is that it's disrespectful to the tradition."

"No, that's not really it. I don't care about the tradition. It's just that you might look foolish, Martin. And desperate. Don't you see, it's gimmicky, and you've never been one for gimmicks."

"For Christ's sake, Judith, don't make too

much of it. It's just a teaching aid."

The children have turned from the television now and are watching us. Grandpa Gill and Lala, almost imperceptibly, shrink away from us.

"Martin, you've always been so sensible. Can't you see that this is just, well, just a little undignified. I mean, I just feel it's beneath you somehow."

"I don't see what's so undignified about trying something new for a change. Christ, Judith. You're the one who thinks the seventeenth century is such a bore. Literature can be damn dull. And especially Milton."

"I agree. I agree."

"What I'm doing is making a pictorial presentation of themes which will give a quick comprehensive vision of the total design. It's quite simple and straightforward."

"Couldn't you just do a paper on it?"

"No. No, I could not."

"Why not?"

"How can you put a design image into prose?"

"What about that paper they turned down. Couldn't you do that one over for them?"

"No."

"So instead you've dreamed up this lunatic scheme."

"Judith, we're talking in circles. I don't think it's all that idiotic. What do you think, Dad?"

Grandpa Gill regards me. Clearly he does not want to join in the foray, but he is being pressed. He speaks cautiously: "I think I partially understand what Judith is worried about. The publish-or-perish syndrome does occasionally have the effect of forcing academics to make asses of themselves. But, on the other hand, cross-disciplinary approaches seem to be 'well thought of at the moment. A graphic demonstration of a literary work, with the design features stressed, might make quite an interesting presentation if —"

I interrupt, out of exasperation, for I know he can go on in this vein for hours. "Look, Martin there's another thing. And I hate to say this because it sounds so narrow-minded and conventional, but I, well, the truth is — I can't bear to think of you sitting there in your office weaving away. I mean — do you know what I mean? — do you — don't you think it's just a little bit — you know — ?"

"Effeminate?" he supplies the word.

"Eccentric. It's the sort of thing Furlong Eberhardt might dream up."

"And I suppose you think that reference will guarantee instant dismissal of the whole idea."

"Oh, Martin, for heaven's sake, do what you want. I just hate you to look ridiculous."

"To whom? To you?"

"Forget it. I don't even know why we're discussing it." I start picking up newspapers and gathering together the coffee cups. Lala springs to my side, but I tell her not to bother; I can manage.

I feel strange as I carry the cups into the kitchen. A nervy dancing fear is spinning in my stomach, and I lean on the sink for support. A minute ago I had been overjoyed that Martin's wool was to be put to so innocent a purpose. What has happened? What am I afraid of?

Guilt presses; I should have been more consoling when his paper was turned down. I should take greater interest in his work. Year after year he sweats out the required papers and what interest do I show? I proofread them, take out commas, put his footnotes in order. And that's it. No wonder he's developed a soft spot on the brain. To conceive of this bit of madness, actually to carry it through.

And to carry it out furtively, covertly. For I am certain he deliberately withheld the project from me. Perhaps from everyone else as well. He probably even pulls the curtains in his office and locks the door when he weaves. I try to picture it — Martin tugging at the wool, sorting his needles, tightening his frame, and then pluck, pluck, in and out, in and out. My husband, Martin Gill, weaving away his secret afternoons.

It might even be better if he did have a mistress. One could understand that. One could commiserate; one could forgive. But what can be done with a man who makes a fool of himself — what do you do then?

Martin is crazy. He's lost his grip. Or is it me? I try to think logically, but my stomach is seized by pain. I try to construct the past few months, to remember exactly when Martin last mentioned something about his work. I sit down on the kitchen stool and try to concentrate, but my head whirls. When did he last discuss the seventeenth century? *Paradise Lost*? The Milton tradition? Or something temporal such as his lecture schedule. When? I can't remember.

And then I think with a stab of pain, when did we last make love with anything more than cordiality?

My head pounds. I open the cupboard and find a bottle of aspirin. And then, though it is just a little past noon, I creep upstairs and get into bed. The sheets are cool and deliciously flat. Below me in the family room I can hear the Rose Bowl Game beginning.

Hours later I awake in the darkened room. In the upstairs hall the light is burning brutally; long, startling El Greco shadows cut across the bedroom wall. Footsteps, whispers, the rattle of teacups. Someone reaches for my hand, places a cold cloth on my forehead.

"Thank you, thank you," I want to say, but my voice has disappeared, in its place a dry cracked nut of pain. My lips have split; I can taste blood. The inside of my mouth is unfamiliar, a clutch of cottonwood.

"Drink this," someone says.

"No, no," I rasp.

"Please, Judith. Try. It may help."

Lala was sitting on the edge of my bed, a figurine, a blue-tinted shepherdess. She was pressing a teaspoon toward me. I opened my mouth. Aspirin. Aspirin crushed in strawberry jam; its peculiar bitter, slightly citrus flavour reaches me from the forest of childhood (my father crushing aspirin on the breadboard with the back of a teaspoon when my sister and I had measles, yes).

A drink of water, and I lay back exhausted. Again the cool, wet cloth. Again the mellifluous voice. "There, there. Now just sleep. Don't worry. Just rest, dear."

What choice had I but to obey; the lack of choice, the total surrender of will enclosed me like a drag. I slept.

There followed another long blurred space.

Several times I woke up choking on the thick cactus growth in my throat. And to my inexplicable grief every time I opened my eyes it was still dark. If only it were light, I remember thinking, I could bear it. If only this long night would end, I would be all right.

But when the light finally did come, milky through the frosted-over windows, I couldn't look at it without pain. It battered my stripped nerve ends, pierced me through with its harsh squares. Anguish. To be so helpless. The wet plush tongue of the facecloth descended again. Coolness. It was Meredith.

In all her sixteen years I had never heard such sadness in her voice. It curled in and out of her breath like a ballad.

"Mother. Oh, Mother. Are you any better?"

Was that my voice that squawked "yes"? I said it to comfort her, not because it was true.

"The doctor's coming. Dr. Barraclough is coming. Any minute, Mother. After his hospital rounds. He said as soon after ten as he could make it."

I moaned faintly, involuntarily.

"Is there anything you'd like, Mother? A nice cup of tea?"

In my angle of pain I could only think of what a strange phrase that was for Meredith to use — a nice cup of tea. Did I ever say it? My mother certainly did. Lala did too. Even Martin did. But did I?

Out of kindness or ritual or sympathy did I ever in all my life offer anyone such a thing as a "nice cup of tea"? If not, then how did I come to have a daughter who was able to utter, unself-consciously, such a perfect and cottagy phrase — *a nice cup of tea?*

Her voice rocked with such mourning that I felt I must accept. From the roof of my mouth a small scream escaped, saying "Yes please."

She fled to the kitchen joyfully, only to be replaced by Martin. "My poor Judith. My poor little Judith."

Again it was the phrase I perceived, not the situation. "My poor little Judith," he had called me. Echoes of courtship, when he had used those exact words often. And I am not little. Tall and lanky then, I am tall and large now, not fat, of course, only what the world calls a fair-sized woman; my size has always defined my sense of myself, made me less serious, freer of vanity, for good or bad.

"My poor little Judith," he had said. I reached out a hand and felt it taken.

"Poor Judith. My poor sick Judith."

So that was it: I was sick.

"Just try to rest, love. You've got some kind of flu. And you've had a bugger of a night."

I strangled with agreement.

"Mother and Dad had to leave. Early this morning. They were awfully worried, especially Mother."

I thought of Lala sitting on the edge of my bed in some half-blocked fantasy. Aspirin and strawberry jam. We had met at that level. I clutched Martin's hand harder. I wanted him to stay and, miraculous, he didn't hurry away.

Richard poked his head around the doorway. I was shocked at his size, for viewed from this unfamiliar angle, he seemed suddenly much taller. A stranger. And miserably shy.

"Meredith says, do you want some toast?"

"No," I croaked. Then I added, "No thank you." Etiquette. My mother's thin etiquette surfacing.

I fell asleep again, woke momentarily to see the tea, cold and untouched in its pottery cup. Sleep, sleep.

The doctor comes. A provincial tennis champion, now barely thirty-five. Too young to wield such power. Permanently suntanned from all those holidays in the Bahamas, hands lean across the backs, a look of cash to his herringbone jacket. Money rolling in, but who cares, who cares?

"Well, well, what have we here?" he whistles good cheer.

Sullenly I refuse to answer or even listen to such heartiness.

He does the old routine, listens to heart — is my nightgown clean? — temperature, pulse, blood pressure. A searing little light with a cold metal tip pokes into throat, nostrils, ears. Eyelids rolled back.

"You're sick," he says leaning back. "A real sick girl."

And you're a fatuous ass, I long to say, but how can I, for he and only he can deliver me from my width of wretchedness. Already he is writing something on a pad of paper. I can — I can be restored.

He speaks to Martin; perhaps he considers that I am too ill to comprehend. "I can only give her something to make her more comfortable. It's a virus, you know, a real tough baby, it looks like, and there's nothing we can give for a virus."

"Nothing?" Martin asks unbelieving.

"Rest, plenty of liquids, that's about it."

"But how about an antibiotic or something?"

"Won't work," he says, brushing Martin off — how dare he! — picking up his overcoat, feeling in his pocket for his car keys.

Meredith sees him to the door, and Martin and I are left in immense quiet. The Baby Ben is ticking on the night table. In spite of my contagious condition, Martin lies down on his side of the rumpled bed. He lies carefully on top of the bedspread and in less than a minute he has fallen asleep.

I am obscurely angered that he has violated my bed with his presence. The walls dissolve, the silence is enormous. I think, *I can't bear this.* And then I too fall asleep.

For days the fever laps away at me. My scalp, after a week, feels so tender that I can hardly comb my hair. My arms and legs ache, and my back is so sore that I keep an extra pillow under it.

The efforts of Martin and the children to comfort me are so great and so constant that I wish I could rouse myself to gratitude. But it is too tiring. I can do nothing but lie in bed and accept.

I have never in my adult life been so ill. I can hardly believe I am suffering from something as ubiquitous as flu, and it seems preposterous that I can be this ill and still not require hospitalization. The doctor comes once again, pats me roughly on the back and says, "Well, Judith, I think you're going to surprise us and weather this after all."

My illness shocks me by giving me almost magical powers of perception; the restless, feverish days have sharpened my awareness to the point of pain. Phrases I hear every day acquire new meaning. I find myself analyzing for hours what is casually uttered. The way, for instance, that Dr. Barraclough calls me Judith now that I have become an author. All sorts of people, in fact, whom I know in a remote and professional way began using my first name the moment my first book came out, as though I had somehow come into the inheritance of it, as though I had entered into the public domain, had left behind that dumpy housewife, Mrs. Gill. *Judith.* I became Judith.

And Meredith who has called me Mother for years is suddenly calling me Mommy again. I lie here in bed, a sick doll, my limbs helpless, living on asparagus soup, and am called Mommy by my sixteen-year-old daughter.

Another observation. Richard doesn't call me anything. He pokes his head in, sometimes even sits for a minute on the edge of the bed. "Would you like the newspaper?" he will ask. Or "Do we have any postage stamps? Any airletters?" But these statements, requests, questions have, I notice, a bald quality. I analyze them. I have time to analyze them. What gives them their flat spare sound is the lack of any salutation. I ponder the reasons. Is he caught in that slot of growth where Mommy is too childish, Mother too severe and foreign? What did he use to call me? When he was little? Now that I think of it, did he ever call me anything? I can't remember. It's curious. And worrying in an obscure way which I am unable, because of my present weakness or because of a prime failing, to understand.

After ten days I began to stay awake longer. The nights lost their nightmare quality, and the joints in my body tormented me less. I was cheered by a letter from my sister and wryly amused by another from my mother. Martin had phoned to tell her I was sick; she was not to worry if she didn't get her weekly letter. Her letter to me was a harping scold from beginning to end. I did too much, she wrote. I wore myself out, wore my fingers to the bone. I should get Martin to take over more of the household chores. Meredith should be washing dishes at her age, and there was no reason she couldn't take over the ironing. Richard could be more helpful too. But basically, I was at fault. I had done too much Christmas entertaining, she accused. Too much shopping, sent too many cards. I shouldn't have invited Martin's parents for New Year's; they had a home of their own, didn't they? And very comfortable too. And why didn't Martin's sister in P.E.I. have them for a change. I should forget about my biographies until the children were older and off my hands.

I read it all, shaking my head. It had always been that way. My sister and I had been scolded for every scraped knee — "I told you you weren't watching." There were no bright badges of mercurochrome for us — "Next time you'll be more careful." For diarrhea we were rewarded with "Play with the Maddeson children and what do you expect?" Even our childhood illnesses were begrudged us. I thought of Lala spooning aspirin into me on New Year's night. And I recalled the first time I had met her. Martin had taken me home for a weekend to Montreal, and he had mentioned to his mother that he had a slight rash on the back of his hands. "Oh dear," she had cried, "what a bother! That can be so irritating. Now let me see. I think I have just the thing. Just squeeze a little of this on, and if that doesn't work we'll just pop you over to the doctor."

I had listened amazed; such acceptance, such outpouring concern. Such willingness to proffer cups of tea, cream soups, poached eggs on toast. Imagine!

And so, although I lie suffering in my arms, legs, stomach, sinus, throat, skin, ears, eyes and kidneys, I am, at least, free of guilt. It is incredible, but no one with the exception of my mother — and she is far away in her multihued bungalow in Scarborough — no one blames me for being sick. Indeed, they almost seem to believe that I am entitled to an illness; that I have earned the right to take to my bed.

I heard Meredith talking to Gwendolyn on the telephone, her voice arched with pride, saying that I had never been sick before. And when Roger dropped in one evening to bring me an armful of magazines, Martin told him in a somewhat self-congratulatory tone, "First time in her life that Judith's been hit like this."

The children went back to school early in January, and Martin too had to go back to the university. But he left me only for his lectures, spending the rest of the time at home. It was curious, the two of us in the house together day after day, reminiscent almost of our early married years when he had been a graduate student and we had lived a close, intimate and untidy apartment life with no special hours for meals or bedtimes; our rituals were in their infancy then.

He works at the little card table in our bedroom where I usually work. Because he is here so much and because my sinuses hurt too much for me to read, I find myself locked into an absorbing meditation with Martin, my husband Martin, at its centre. Endlessly I think about him and the shape his life has taken and about the curious but not disagreeable distance that has grown between us. My days of fever confer on me a ferocious insight, and I find I can observe Martin with a startling new, almost X-ray vision.

Martin. Martin Gill, I try to define you, and since I've no machinery, no statistical tools, I do it the easy way, by vocation — but you know yourself how little vocation defines anyone. I play categories; I take the number of universities in this province — it's about ten, isn't it? — and divide that number into departments, allowing about one-twelfth of any university involved in the teaching of English language and literature. And then I divide that in six, allowing for Am. Lit., Can. Lit., Anglo-Saxon, Elizabethan, Victorian, Mods — better make that about one-seventh in Renaissance, and there — I have you pinned down, Martin. You see, you are statistically definable, but where do we go from here? Isolate the Renaissance group and ask, how many of them are in their early forties, own a house with a still sizable mortgage, are married to largish wives with intellectual (but not really) leanings. And children. Children with the usual irritations but, thank God, cross yourself unbeliever though you be, no mongoloids, no cleft palates, no leaky hearts, leukemia, no fatal automobile accidents, no shotgun weddings, no drug charges, just two normal children, and we do love them, don't we Martin?

Once, about ten years or so ago, I came

across a pile of Martin's lecture notes. And scribbled in the margin were clusters of scribbled notations in his handwriting. "Explain in depth." "Draw parallel with Dante." "Explain cosmos — the idea at the time — use diagram." "Joke about Adam's rib — ask, is it relevant?" "Stress!!!" "Question for understanding of original sin." "Don't push this point — alien concept." "What would Freud say about this response?" "Ask for conclusions at this point — sum up."

They were messages. Messages partly cryptic, partly illuminating, the little knobs upon which he hung his communications, notations to himself. *Did I write messages to myself? What were they?* Martin's fringe of marginal notes and messages reminded me — yes, I admitted it — reminded me that he possessed an existence of his own to which I did not belong, which I did not understand and which — be truthful now, Judith — which I did not really want to understand.

On Martin's side of the family, no one has the slightest degree of mechanical ability. His grandfather never even learned to drive a car, and his father cannot do the simplest household repairs; he is even somewhat vain about his lack of dexterity. A handyman, a Mr. Henshawe who is almost a family retainer, comes regularly to change washers, rehang doors, even to install cuphooks.

It is only natural that Martin has inherited the family ineptness — how could it be otherwise? — but unlike his father, it is not a source of pride with him. Handymen are expensive and unreliable nowadays, and professors do not earn large salaries. I suspect he would like to be able to fix the water heater or put up bookshelves himself. When he looks at Richard he must see that his son will be heir to his inabilities and subject to his niggling expenses. What does he think then?

About three years ago Martin came home with a small flat box from the Hudson's Bay Company. I was making a salad in the kitchen, and I glanced at the box hopefully, thinking that he might have bought me a gift as he sometimes does. "What's that?" I asked, slicing into a tomato.

He folded back a skin of tissue paper and lifted out a small bow tie, a small crimson silky bowtie, and held it aloft as though it were a model aircraft, rotating it slowly for my inspection.

I was so astonished I could only gasp, "What is it?"

"A tie."

"But who is it for?"

"For me," he said, smiling and holding it under his chin.

"But you've never worn a bow tie."

"That's where you're wrong. I wore one for years. A red one. Just like this. Every Friday night at the school dance."

"But Martin, that was back in the days when people wore bow ties."

"They're making a comeback. The man at the Bay said so."

"I can't see you in it," I said. "I just can't see you actually wearing a thing like that."

And he never did. When I straighten his top drawer I always see that same flat Hudson's Bay box, and inside is the bow tie still in its tissue paper. When I see it I can't help but speculate about the moment that prompted him to buy it, but the impulses of others are seldom understandable; they seem to spring out of irrational material, out of the dark soil of the subconscious. But I have respect for impulses and for the mystery they suggest. Even the madness they hint at. That's why I have never mentioned the tie to Martin again. I just straighten his drawer and put everything back neatly and then shut it again.

Why then can't I shut out the wool?

Martin Gill, B.A., M.A., Ph.D. (with distinction)

Age — forty-one

Appearance — somewhat boyish. Never handsome but has been described as agreeable looking, pleasant; his greatest physical charm springs from a slow-motion smile (complete with good-looking eye crinkles, dimple on left cheek, decent teeth) and accompanied by rough-tumbling tenor laugh.

Profession — Associate Professor of English. Specialty — Milton.

Politics — Leftish, Fabianish, believes socialism is "cry of anguish." Like his father, grandfather, etc. Milton would have been a socialist, he believes, if he were alive now. He has made this remark, at the most, three times. He is not a man who is "given" to certain expressions.

Likes — simple things (one friend calls him Martin the Spartan). Reads newspapers, a few magazines, anything written before 1830 and a selection of contemporary writings. Also likes family, friends, a good meal, a good beer, a good laugh, a well-told story, a touchdown or a completed pass, Scrabble (if he is winning), sex (especially in the morning and with a minimum of acrobatics), children (his own exclusively), a clean bathroom in which to take a vigorous shower with very hot water.

Prospects — getting older. More of

same. One or perhaps two more promotions, continued fidelity.

Susanna Moodie always called her husband Moodie. His name was John Wedderburn Dunbar Moodie, but she called him Moodie, and I frequently wonder how a woman could love a man she called Moodie. But she must have loved him, at least at first. I am reminded of a girl I knew at university, a small, rodent-faced girl, excessively intellectual and rather nasty, named Rosemary, who was majoring in modern poetry and who, when I told her I was going to marry Martin Gill, said, "How could anyone fuck a Milton specialist?"

Martin has a touching respect for modern technology, regarding it as a cult practised by priests in another dimension of human intelligence.

Once when our car was still new, we were driving in an ice storm, and he turned on the defrost button. Together we watched a semicircle of glass mysteriously clear itself; soft, moist breath came out of nowhere, ready at the touch of a button to lick through the ice. "Wonderful," he murmured, smiling his slow smile. He shook his head and said it again, "Wonderful."

Another time we phoned to Canada from

England. I stood with him in the cramped and freezing corner callbox. The operator said, "Just a minute, love," and somehow the wires obeyed. Voices actually filtered through, recognizable voices from across the ocean. He could hardly believe it. He held the receiver a little away from him and regarded it with wonder. "God," he said to me, "can you believe it?"

And flying home to Canada in the gigantic jet he watched out the window as the wing flaps went through their taking off performance. The wheels rushed under the floor, a stewardess passed out chewing gum; everything seemed wonderfully orchestrated; even the no-smoking signs blinked in time and a quartet of lissome stewardesses demonstrated an oxygen mask in the aisle, stylized as a ballet. When we were aloft with the green fields curving beneath us, Martin looked out the window, incredulous, almost mad with joy, gripping my hand. "What do you think of that?" he whispered.

The little battery shaver I gave him for Christmas holds magic for him. He cups it in his hand, loving its compressed and secret energy. The timing mechanism of my oven delights him, and he likes to think of the blue waterfalls performing inside the dishwater. Sometimes I think he has not quite caught up to this age, that he is hanging back a little on purpose out of some mysterious current in his disposition which hungers for miracles.

I am still sick. Not in a state of suffering as I was, but exhausted. The least effort is too much for me. Yesterday I got up to look for a library book, and after a moment's searching I collapsed back into bed. It wasn't worth it; I am too tired to read anyway.

In the mornings I lie in bed listening to the radio. The melange of music, news spots and interviews soothes; it is a monotonous droning, familiar and comforting; it demands nothing of me. I welcome passivity.

One morning Martin climbed back into bed with me. We scanned the newspapers together and then lay back to listen to the radio. We heard some funny tunes from the Forties, an interview with an ecologist whose passion leaked out over the airwaves, a theatre review, another interview, this one quite funny. I noticed that Martin and I, lying on our backs, laughed in exactly the same places. Almost as though we were reading cue cards. We have never done this before, never lain in bed all morning listening to the radio, laughing together. The novelty of it is striking. It comes as a surprise. And it is all the more surprising because I had thought there could be no more surprises.

Martin fell in love with me because of my vivacity, or so he says, which would mean that he at forty-one is sadly swindled. Perhaps he didn't understand that what he took to be vivacity was only a gust of nervous energy which surfaced in my early twenties, a reaction probably to the cartoon tidiness of Scarborough. Whatever it was, it has more or less drained away, appearing only occasionally in lopsided, frenetic moments. But I can still, if I try, conjure it up. I can charm him still, make him look at me with love. But it requires a tremendous effort of the will. Concentration. Energy. And that may eventually go too. People change, and I suppose everyone has to accept that.

I've noticed, for instance, something about my mother, who all her married life busied herself redecorating her six small rooms in Scarborough; plaster, paint, paper, varnish, they were her survival equipment. But when my father died, a quiet death, a heart attack in his sleep, she stopped decorating. The house seemed to fall away from her. She still lives there, of course, but there is no more fresh paint, no newly potted plants; she has not even rearranged the furniture since he died. And though I know this must be significant and that it must in some way say something about their life together, I am reluctant to dwell on the reasons. I want to push it away from me like Martin's plans to reproduce *Paradise Lost* in wool. (He has not mentioned it since New Year's Day; he has, in fact, very carefully avoided it. And so have I.)

I am feeling well enough to have visitors. Nancy Krantz came one day bringing a chicken casserole for the family, and for me, a new Iris Murdoch novel, expensively hard-covered and just exactly what I had yearned for.

Roger Ramsay brought us a bottle of his homemade wine, and he and Martin and I sit one evening in the bedroom sipping it, I in my most attractive dressing gown, propped up by pillows. But to my tender throat the wine is excruciatingly acidic.

Roger is despondent; his blue jean jacket hangs mournfully from his shoulders, and his hair falls in his eyes. It seems he and Ruthie have quarreled and that she has left him. Where has she gone? I ask him. He doesn't know. He phones the library where she works every day, but she refuses to speak to him. What is the problem? I ask. He shrugs. He isn't sure.

I find I cannot join into his depression. Three weeks in bed have made me incapable of sympathy. Besides I cannot believe

Ruthie would leave him for good.

We sip wine and talk; it's only nine-thirty and already I'm wearing down. Martin notices, and I see him signal Roger that it's time to go. He stands up awkwardly, buttons his denim jacket, kisses my hand with such gentleness that I feel tears standing in my eyes. Poor Roger.

Ruthie doesn't come to see me, but she sends a basket of fruit and a card saying only: "Jude, take care. I love you, Ruthie."

Furlong brings a huge and expensive book of photographs. $21.50. He has neglected to detach the price. *Canada: Its future and Its Now*, the sort of book I seldom pick up. But it's somehow perfect for convalescence. And his mother sends along a jar of red currant jelly which is the first good thing I've tasted all month. She made it herself and poured it into this graceful pressed-glass jar. Meredith spreads it on toast every day and brings it with a pot of tea before she leaves for school. She brings bread from our favourite Boston Bakery which means she walks an extra two miles. I could weep.

Richard lends me his portable record player and from his allowance he buys me a new LP. Stravinsky. He has grown shy. He doesn't quite look me in the eye, but he talks about "when you get better" as though all things of worth hinge on that condition.

Martin is attentive. Unfailing. Why am I so surprised? Is it because he's not been tested before? He sets up my typewriter on the bed one day when I feel that I've neglected Susanna Moodie long enough.

Susanna. I've reached a place in her life where she makes, with a single imaginative stroke, an attempt to rescue herself, an attempt to alter her life. It is the single anomaly of her life, an enormous biographical hiatus, a time-fold, a geological faultline which remains visible for the rest of her life.

Bizarre though it may seem today, her single decisive act proceeded directly out of the skein of her desperation, and it's possible that her intercession wasn't all that remarkable in the context of her time.

The situation couldn't have been worse. John Moodie, Susanna's husband had botched it as a farmer; not his fault perhaps, for the sort of gentlemanly farming he had envisioned was simply not possible in the Canadian bush. But he had gone down with a deplorable lack of style, and comes across as a limping, whining man, a poor loser, dogged by misfortune, the sort of misfortune which is almost invited. He sold his only possession, a military commission, and squandered the money on worthless steamboat stock. Although Susanna tried gamely to lighten his portrait here and there by referring to his flute playing, his literary discourse, his attempts at writing, he is ever sour and irritable and heavy-footed, not a man to grow old and mellow with.

By 1837 he admitted that he had failed as a backwoodsman; he was in debt; his wife was expecting her fifth child, and winter was coming. Their condition was deteriorating rapidly when they received word that a rebellion had broken out in Toronto. Almost all the able-bodied men in the neighbourhood, including John Moodie, were called away to fight, and the prospect of regular pay was greeted with joy. Moodie sent home some of his money to Susanna who used it to pay off debts. Alone all winter with her children and a hired girl, she had a chance to reflect on the family prospects. She too admitted the farm had been a mistake. Worse still, Moodie wrote that the rebellion was over and the regiment was about to be disbanded; he would soon be without pay again.

Driven nearly to madness, Susanna sat down and wrote a long confessional and impassioned letter to Sir George Arthur who was the Lieutenant-Governor of Upper Canada, outlining the series of disasters that had befallen the family and begging him to keep her husband on in the militia. Her efforts were rewarded, for Moodie was soon made Paymaster to the Militia and later appointed Sheriff of the District of Victoria.

The letter is astonishing enough; but even more extraordinary is the fact that John Moodie never knew about it. He speculated that he was probably awarded the paymaster position because of his exemplary sobriety while in the militia. And the office of sheriff because of his honest performance as paymaster.

It seems almost beyond belief that the story of the letter never leaked out, that Susanna herself never once in all those years let slip to her husband the true cause of his sudden elevation in society. Or was John Moodie bluffing? It is a possibility; to save face he may have neglected to mention the enormous step his wife took to save him. But it is just as possible, even probable, that she kept her secret, kept it all her life, either to spare his pride or to avoid seeming too much the schemer.

They were a married couple, shared a bed, faced each other over a supper table well into old age — all this with a secret between them. Secrets. I never did tell Martin that I had read John Spalding's manuscripts. He would not have liked it; he would have looked at me with less than love; it might even have damaged the balance between us. And he, for perhaps the same reason, put off telling me about the woollen tapestries. He must have guessed how I would react. Secrets are possible. And between people who love each other, maybe even necessary.

One night I woke at one o'clock. I had been asleep for two hours; the house was deathly quiet, and beside me, Martin was breathing deeply. I sat up and wondered what had wakened me so suddenly and so completely. A loud noise? a branch breaking? an icicle falling? a burglar? I listened. There was nothing but a faint gnawing of wind. I got out of bed and went over to the window. There everything was serene; the curving road was touched with ice-blue shadows. The street light poured a steady milk-white light on the snow, beautiful.

Then I realized what it was that had wakened me: I was well. I was restored to health. In the complicated subknowledge of my body chemistry, health had been reannounced. A click like an electric switch marked the end of illness. I stretched with health, with a feeling almost of being reborn. Strength, joy.

I had been sick almost a whole month, enclosed in the wide, white parentheses of weakness, part of a tableau of trays and orange juice and aspirin tablets. I had inhabited a loop of time, been assaulted by an uneasy coalition of suffering and perception, and now I was to be released.

Outside the window, possibility sparkled on every bush and tree. My household was asleep; in dark caves my husband and children dreamed. Heat puffed up from the basement furnace and entered every corner of the house. In the kitchen marvellous things lay on shelves, delicate and tempting. The refrigerator held the unspeakable pleasures of bacon and eggs. I was starved.

Downstairs I switched on a light, blinded at first by the brightness. I found a frying pan and butter, lots of butter, and humming I prepared my feast. And ate it all, believing that nothing had ever tasted so good before.

Thoughts stormed through my head, plans, what I would do tomorrow, the next day, the next. I paced. There was no point in going back to bed in this state. I poked in the family room for old magazines, something, anything to read.

Graven Images lay upside down on the arm of the green chair where Meredith had left it. Furlong glinted at me from the back cover. I picked it up thinking, why not see what it's about. This was the perfect time.

I slung myself on the sofa, my feet dragging over one end, my dressing gown pulled around me, for I was beginning to feel chilly. And the greyness of fatigue was making my head ache. But I opened the book and began to read.

I went through the first chapter quickly, irritated by the familiar Eberhardt style. But I went on to the second chapter anyway, proceeding through waves of boredom into shock, incredulity, anger. I finished the last chapter at dawn, at seven o'clock, a thin nervous time, my whole body chilled with disbelief and dull accumulated rage. How could you, Furlong!

My heart was beating wildly; I could feel it through the heavy quilting of my dressing gown. Anger almost choked me, but in spite of it (or maybe even because of it), I fell instantly asleep where I was, cramped on the sofa with *Graven Images* upside down on my chest.

February

"These severe cases of flu are almost always followed by depression," Dr. Barraclough warned me. "Watch out not to get too tired or emotionally overwrought. Just sit back, Judith. No running around. And above all," he warned, "no worrying."

But the minute I was on my feet, the solicitude around me evaporated. Meredith's morning trays came to a halt and Richard took back his record player. Martin woke me at seven-thirty sharp to make breakfast. If it hadn't been for Frieda who came once a week to clean the house, we would have fallen apart completely. For I *was* tired. I *was* depressed; the world did indeed seem lull of obscure threatening dangers, treacheries, mean cuts and thrusts, insults briskly traded, conniving jealousies, nursed grudges, selfish hang-ups, greed, opportunism, ego, desperation and stupidity; in addition, I felt too weary to cope with the overpowering, wounding and private betrayal of *Graven Images*.

I dragged through the first week of February alternating between rage and depression, sore to the bone and overwhelmed by exhaustion. Furlong Eberhardt and his casual treason plucked at me hourly. I could not forget it for a minute. I had been used. Used by a friend. Taken advantage of. Furlong who had been trusted (although not always loved) had stolen something from me, and that act made him both thief and enemy.

So simply, so transparently, and so unapologetically had he stolen the plot for *Graven Images* — stolen it from me who had in turn stolen it from John Spalding who — it occurred to me for the first time — might have stolen it from someone else. The chain of indictment might stretch back infinitely, crime within crime within crime.

But the fact remained that it was Furlong who had actually gone through with it. A nefarious, barefaced theft. I had at least resisted temptation; and although it had not been the thought of plagiarism which had deterred me, but rather the inability to reconcile the real with the unreal — "that willing suspension of disbelief" when the moment required — still I had resisted, and that resistance bestowed on me a species of innocence. I was no more than a neutral party, a mere agent of transfer. On the other hand, was corruption transferable by simple infection?

I preferred not to think about it; large

abstract problems of sin have never been my specialty. It is the casual treason between individuals, the miniature murders of sensibility which chew away at me, and what Furlong had done was to help himself to something that had been mine. That it hadn't been mine in the first place was immaterial, for as far as he knew the plot had been my idea, my conception, my child.

Would it have mattered, I asked myself, if he had told me, or if he had asked permission; if he had perhaps suggested that, since I wasn't interested in developing the idea myself, would I mind terribly if he more or less appropriated it? Would I have smiled, gracious at such a request? Would I have said, of course, help yourself, someone might as well have the use of it, as though it were a pound of hamburger he was borrowing or the use of my typewriter?

I doubt it. I'm too possessive, and besides I would then have had to confess my theft from John Spalding. And the thought of John Spalding was beginning to weigh on me. Furlong, after all, had done quite well with the sales of *Graven Images*. It was, in fact, selling better than any of his previous books for the simple reason that it was better than any of the others. And there was no doubt about the reason for that: it was the first book he had ever written which contained anything like a structure, a structure which was derived from a plot which he had stolen, which he had acquired (to use horse-breeders' jargon) by me out of John Spalding.

Not only were his royalties promising, but he had sold the film rights for what Martin assured me must be a handsome figure. He was going to benefit enormously, while John Spalding, in contrast, sat tormented and constipated in Birmingham, lusting for recognition and trying to stretch his lecturer's salary, month by meagre month, to cover the cheapest existence he could devise: bacon dripping on his bread, I imagined, and doing his own repairs on the third-hand Morris, tripe and onion instead of Sunday joint, and smoking his Woodbines down to their frazzled ends. It was monumentally unjust.

Of course I realized I would have to confront Furlong; it was unthinkable to let this pass. But for that I needed strength. I would have to wait until I was stronger. The phrase "girding my loins" occurred to me. I would need to arm myself, for I was still weak, hardly able to cook a meal without flopping exhausted back into bed. And for reasons which Dr. Barraclough might recognize, I was continually on the verge of weeping.

Tears stood like pin pricks in the backs of my eyes. I was prepared to cry over anything. Martin called from the university to say he would be staying late to work. He didn't say what he would be working on, but we both knew; and when I thought of him in his cork-walled solitude, selecting and blending his wools, threading his needles and weaving away, woof and warp, in and out, I wanted to sob with anguish.

Meredith encloses herself in her room. She is re-reading all of Furlong's books, and our copy of *Graven Images* has been marked and underlined. Exclamation points stand in the margins, the corners of pages have been turned under to indicate her favourite passages. She listens to music and reads and reads. Her loneliness and the sort of love she is imagining tears at me, but there is nothing I can do but leave her to her disk jockeys and the comfort of printed pages.

And I bleed for Richard. There was no letter for him this week. He could hardly believe it at first. Then we read about the postal strike in Britain, and he breathed with relief. The reason, at least, was known. Circumstances were beyond his immediate control; he would have to wait.

He checks the newspapers daily for news of the strike, mentioning it offhandedly to us so we won't suspect how much he cares or how dependent he has grown on the weekly letters from Anita Spalding. "When the strike ends, there's going to be a real bonanza," he says, picturing the accumulated letters pouring in all at once. The thought sustains him for a while, but then he worries because his letters aren't getting through. Will she understand about the strike? he wonders. Of course, we assure him, how could she not understand? He hears somewhere that top priority mail is trickling through, and he feels obscurely that he deserves to be top priority, that his letters matter.

The strike drags on, and Martin and I suggest things he can do to keep busy. Martin takes him skiing, and in spite of my fatigue I help him with a school project on Tanzania. We trace maps; I type an agricultural output chart for him. He has taken to sighing heavily.

Even Susanna Moodie has let me down. I am writing now about her later life when she has moved with her husband and children to the town of Belleville. No longer destitute, she has grown cranky. She says unkind things about the neighbouring women. She minimizes the efforts of the town builders; she has lost the girlish excitement and breathless gaiety which made life in the bush cabin seem an adventure; the glory of fresh raspberries and the thrill of milking a cow are forgotten pleasures. She is a matron now, and she makes hard, grudging judgments. She has lost her vision. She is condescending. The action goes too fast; she telescopes five years into a maddening paragraph. There are no details anymore.

It would help if it snowed. The ground is covered with old crusted snow and pitted with ice. The roads and sidewalks are rutted and hard to walk on, and driving is dangerous. A layer of grime covers everything. One soft and lovely fall of snow might at least keep me from this overwhelming compulsion to put my head down and cry and cry and cry.

I don't really feel like cooking, but I feel so sorry for Roger that one night we invite him for a family dinner. He hasn't heard from Ruthie. He doesn't know where she's living. He would feel better, he tells me, if he knew where she was staying.

"Are you really that worried about her?" I ask, putting a slice of meatloaf on his plate.

"No. I know she's all right because she's at work."

"What then?"

"I just want to know where she's living."

"You've tried her girl friends?"

"Yes. And they don't know."

"What about her family?" I ask. I know she is from a small town in northern Ontario. "Couldn't you write to them?"

"God, no. They never liked the idea that we were living together. Not married. They're pretty rigid."

"Why don't you follow her home from work?" Richard asks, taking the words out of my mouth.

"Don't be stupid," Meredith says sternly. "This isn't a James Bond movie. That would be just plain sneaky, following her like that."

I say nothing. Roger shakes his head sadly. "I couldn't. Believe me, I've thought about it, but it does seem to be an invasion — and, I don't know — I just couldn't."

Martin interrupts us with, "Look, if she wants it this way, isn't it better to leave her alone. You've got to get your mind on something else, Roger."

"God knows I'm busy enough at work," Roger says. "It seems I've just got the Christmas exams marked, and now we're onto a new set. I don't even have time to do enough reading to keep up."

"What did you think of *Graven Images?*" I ask him suddenly.

"Great." He barks it out. "Absolutely his best."

"Why?" I ask, trying not to sound too sly.

"I don't know, Judith. It's got more — more body to it."

"A better plot?" I suggest.

"That's it. A real brainstorm. No wonder the films snatched it up."

"I just loved it," Meredith murmurs.

Martin says nothing; he still hasn't got around to reading it.

"Tell me, Roger," I ask, "would you say that Furlong is an original writer?"

"Damn right I would."

"How is he original?" I ask. "Tell me, in what way is he original?"

Roger leans back, shaking his thick curls out of his eyes, and for a moment Ruthie is forgotten, for a moment he seems happy. He is recalling phrases from his thesis. "All right, Judith, take his use of the Canadian experience. Now there's a man who actually comprehends the national theme."

"Which is what?" Martin asks.

"Which is shelter. Shelter from the storm of life, to use a corny phrase."

"Corny is right," Richard says.

"Who asked you, Richard?" Meredith tells him.

In the kitchen I serve ice-cream drizzled with maple syrup; I haven't the energy to think of anything else. Meredith carries in the plates for me. Roger is expanding on the theme of shelter.

"I don't, of course, mean just shelter from those natural storms which occur externally. Although he is tremendous on those.

That hail sequence in *Graven Images* — now didn't that grab you? Even you'd like it, Martin. It's got a sort of Miltonic splendour. Like the hail is a symbol. He makes it stand for the general battering of everyday life."

"So what about the shelter theme?" Martin is smiling broadly, happy tonight.

"Okay, I'm getting to that. Remember the guy out on the prairie, Judith, just standing there. And the hail starts. Golfballs. His dog is killed. Remember that?"

"Christ," Martin says. "It sounds like *Lassie Come Home.*"

"It sounds bad, I'll admit. But that's the beautiful thing about Furlong. He can carry it off when no one else can. What someone else makes into a soap opera, he makes part of the national fabric."

"But Roger," I plead, "getting back to originality for a moment, do you really think he comes up with original plots?"

"Well, we don't use that word plot much anymore. Not in modern criticism. But, yes, sure I think he does. You read *Graven Images.* Wasn't that a real heart-stopper?"

"What about the others though?" I ask. "Where do you think he got the ideas for those early books? Did you go into that when you wrote your thesis?"

"I suppose you want me to admit that his stories are a bit on the formula plan.

So, okay, I admit it. But *Graven Images* confirms what I said then — that he's a pretty original guy."

"He really is," Meredith says smiling.

"Hmmmm," Martin says.

I say nothing. I am sitting quiet. Girding my loins. I know that my present weakness is trivial and temporary. Next week, I promise myself, next week I'm going to have it out with Furlong. He's going to have to do some explaining. Or else.

Or else what? Endlessly, silently, I debate the point.

What power do I have over Furlong? Who am I, the far from perfect Judith Gill, to judge him, and how do I hope to chastise him for his dishonesty?

I only want him to know that I know what he did.

Why? What's the point? Why not let it pass?

Because what he's done may be too small a crime to punish, but at the same time it's too large to let go unacknowledged. Talk about scot-free.

Is Furlong a bad man then? A criminal?

No, not bad. Just weak. Complex, intelligent, but weak. I've just discovered how weak. But he has a glaze of arrogance, a coloratura confidence that demands that I respond.

In what way is he weak?

176

Let me explain. When I was about fifteen years old I read a very long and boring novel called *Middlemarch*. By George Eliot yet. I got it from the public library. (All girls like me who were good at school but suffered from miserable girlhoods were sustained for years on end by the resources of the public libraries of this continent.) Not that *Middlemarch* offered me much in the way of escape. It offered little but a rambling plot and quartets of moist, dreary, introspective characters, one of whom was accused by the heroine of having "spots of commonness." I liked that expression, "spots of commonness," and even at fifteen I recognized the symptoms, interpreting them as a familiar social variety of measles.

Furlong suffers more than anyone I know from this exact and debilitating malady. Witness the framed motto he once had in his office, and witness also the abrupt banishment of it. Observe the clichés on his book jacket, remember his cranberry-vodka punch, his petty jealousies of other writers, his dependence on nationality which permits him his big-frog-in-little-pond eminence.

His sophistication is problematically wrought; it's uneven and sometimes, when instinct fails, altogether lacking. He can, for instance, be too kind, too lushly, tropi-

177

cally kind, a kindness too rich and ripe for ordinary friendship. And, in addition, he is uncertain about salad forks, brandy snifters, and how to use the subjunctive; he finds those Steuben glass snails charming and he favours Renoir; he sometimes slips and says supper instead of dinner, and, conversely, in another pose, he slips and says dinner instead of supper; he is spotted, oh, he is uncommonly spotted.

But is he less of a thief for all that?

A thief is a thief is a thief.

Very profound. But don't forget, you stole the plot in the first place.

That was different. I didn't actually go through with it. And I didn't profit from it the way Furlong has profited.

So that's what's bothering you. You're jealous.

No, no, no, no. Not for myself. For Martin maybe. Here is Furlong, enjoying an unearned success. And Martin gets nothing but crazy in the head.

Are there no mitigating circumstances in this theft?

Many. Obviously he was desperate. He admitted that much, letting slip the fact that the well had gone dry. He was on the skids, hadn't had a good idea for two years. Poor man, snagged in literary menopause and sticky with hot flushes. And he *is* nice to his mother. And patient with his students. And always touchingly, tenderly gallant with me, actually thinking of me as a fellow writer, and accepting me, great big-boned Judith Gill, as charming, a really quite attractive woman. And what else? Oh, yes. He has a passionate and pitiable desire to be loved, to be celebrated with expletives and nicknames, to be in the club. And then, an alternating compulsion to draw back, to be insular and exclusive and private. Psychologically he's a mess. I suppose he was driven to theft.

But who does it really harm?

I refuse to answer such an academic question.

Don't you like him at all?

Like him? I do. No, I don't, not now. I suppose I'm fond of him. But no matter how charming he will be in the future, no matter how he disclaims his act of plunder and he will, no matter what amends he may make for it, I will not be moved. I don't know why, but he will never, he will never, he will never be someone I love. Only someone I could have loved.

Nancy Krantz and I went out to lunch one day to celebrate my recovery from the flu. We went to the Prince Lodge where Paul Krantz is a member (and has a charge account) and sat at one of the dark oak tables which are moored like ships on the sea of olive carpet. Around us quiet, dark-suited businessmen in twos and threes talked softly; glasses and silver clinked faintly as though at a great distance.

"Two dry sherries," Nancy told the waiter briskly. I longed to tell her about Furlong's plagiarism, but that was out of the question since it would have necessitated the disclosure of my own theft, not to mention my prying into John Spalding's private manuscripts.

We ordered beef curry, and while we waited we discussed the alternating vibrations which regulate female psychology.

"Up and down," Nancy complained. "A perpetual see-saw ride. Pre-menstrual, post-menstrual. Optimism, pessimism."

I agreed; it did seem that the electricity of life consisted mainly of meaningless fluctuations in mood, so that to enter an era of happiness was to anticipate the next interlude of depression.

"Of course," Nancy said, "there are those occasional little surprises which make it all worthwhile."

"Such as?" I asked.

"The peach," she said. "Did I ever tell you the peach story?"

"No," I said, "never."

So she told me how, last summer, she and Paul and their children, all six of them, had been stalled in heavy traffic. It was a

Friday evening and they were working their way out of the city to get to the cottage sixty miles away. The children were quarrelsome and the weather was murderously humid. In another car stalled next to them, a fat man sat alone at the steering wheel, and on the back seat, plainly visible, was a bushel of peaches. He smiled at the children, and they must have smiled back, for he turned suddenly and reached a fat hand into his basket, carefully selected a peach, and handed it out the window to Nancy.

She took it, she said, instinctively, uttering a confused mew of thanks. Ahead of them a traffic light turned green, and the fat man's car moved away, leaving Nancy with the large and beautiful peach in her hand. It was, she said the largest peach she had ever seen, almost the size of a grapefruit, and its skin was perfect seamless velvet without a single blemish. Paul shouted at her over the noise of the traffic to look out for razor blades, so she turned it over carefully, inspecting it. But the skin was unbroken. And the exact shade of ripeness for eating.

"What did you do with it?" I asked.

"We ate it," Nancy said. "We passed it around. Gently. Like a holy object almost, and we each took big bites of it. Until it was gone. One of the children said something about how strange it was for someone to do that, give us a peach through a car window like that, but the rest of us just sat there thinking about it. All the way to the cottage. A strange sort of peace stuck to us. It was so — so completely unasked for. And so undeserved. And the whole thing had been so quick, just a few seconds really. I was — I don't know why — I was thrilled."

I nodded. I was remembering something that had happened to us, an incident I had almost forgotten. It was perhaps a shade less joyous a story than Nancy's, but the element of mystery had, at the time, renewed something in me.

It had happened, I told Nancy, on our first day in England. We had taken a train from London to Birmingham. Everything was very new and crowded and confused; the train puffing into Birmingham seemed charmingly miniature; the station was glass-roofed and dirty with Victorian arches and tea trolleys and curious newspapers arrayed in kiosks; odd looking luggage, belted and roped, even suitcases made of wicker, were stacked on carts. Martin, the children and I struggled with our own bags, hurrying down the platform, disoriented by the feel of solid ground underfoot, bumped and jostled at every step by people hurrying to board the train we had just left. Passengers pulled down the train windows, leaned out talking to their friends while paper cups of tea changed hands and kisses flew through the air. Children with startling red cheeks, wearing blue gabardine coats, hung onto their mothers' hands. A cheerful scruffiness hung over the station like whisky breath.

And at that moment a short, dark little man stopped directly in front of me and pushed a small brown paper parcel at me. I must have shaken my head to indicate that it wasn't mine, but he pushed it even harder at me, speaking all the time, very rapidly, in a language I didn't recognize. Certainly no species of English; nor was it French or German; it might have been Arabic we speculated later.

I pushed the parcel back at him, but he placed it all the more firmly in my hand, speaking faster and more agitatedly than before. "Come on, Judith," Martin called to me. So clutching my suitcase again as well as the parcel, I followed Martin and the children out into the thin sunshine where we flagged a taxi and drove the mile or two to the Spaldings' flat.

The parcel was forgotten for an hour or more; then someone remembered it. I opened it slowly while the children watched. Inside was a box of stationery. Letter paper. About twenty sheets of it in a not very fresh shade of pale green. There was some sort of pinkish flower at the top of each sheet, and at the bottom of the box there were piles of slightly faded looking envelopes.

For a day or two we speculated on what it could mean. We examined every sheet of paper and looked the box over carefully for identifying marks; we tried to recall the man's appearance and the sound of his voice. "He must have thought you'd left it on the seat in the train," Martin said, and in the end we all agreed that that was the most likely answer, the only sensible conclusion really. But it didn't seem quite enough. The little man had been running on the platform. He had searched the crowd, or so I believed, and for some reason he had selected me. And he had run away again in a state of great excitement. We never thought for a moment that the parcel might have been dangerous since this occurred before the invention of letter bombs, but Richard did suggest we run a hot iron over the sheets of paper in the hope of discovering messages written in invisible ink.

Those first few days in England were so filled with novelty, with odd occurrences and curious sights, that this tiny incident, bizarre as it was, seemed no more than a portion of that larger strangeness, and we soon ceased to talk about it. I even used the writing paper for my first letters home, and when it was all gone I forgot about it. Or almost.

For if it seemed a commonplace enough adventure at the time, it grows more strange, more mysterious as time passes. This afternoon, telling Nancy about it, it seemed really quite wonderful in a way, utterly unique in fact, as though we had accidentally brushed with the supernatural.

And the two of us, stirring sugar into our cups of coffee at the Prince Lodge, smiled. It was after three; the businessmen had crept away without our noticing, back to their conference rooms, to their teak desks and in-trays. Here in the restaurant two waiters fluttered darkly by a sideboard, and in all that space I felt myself lifted to a new perspective: far away it seemed, I could see two women at a table; they are neither happy nor unhappy, but are suspended somewhere in between, caught in a thin, clear, expensive jelly, and they are both smiling, smiling across the table, across the room, smiling past the dark stained panelling, out through the tiny-paned window to the parking lot which is slowly, slowly, filling up with snow, changing all the world to a wide, white void.

"It's over. I just heard it on the news,"

Richard yells. "While I was getting dressed. It's all settled."

"What's settled?" It's early, eight o'clock, and I'm pouring out glasses of orange juice, not quite awake.

"The postal strike."

"The postal strike?"

"You know. In the U.K. Don't you remember?"

"Oh, yes, that's right. Heavens, that's been going on a long time."

"Three weeks."

"Really? Where does the time go?"

He sits down at the table and cuts the top off his boiled egg. Joy makes him violent, and the slice of egg shell skitters to the floor. He leans over to pick it up. "Man, it'll be a real pileup. Three weeks of mail!"

I pour my coffee and sit beside him. "It'll take a while to sort it all out."

"I know."

"I mean, you mustn't expect any mail for a while."

"I know. I know."

"It may be several days. A week even."

"Is there any honey?"

"In the cupboard."

"Say about six days. Today's Tuesday. I should be getting something by next Monday."

"Hmmmmm."

"What do you think? Tuesday at the latest?"

"Maybe, but don't count on it."

"Don't worry about me."

He managed to get through the week, casting no more than a casual eye at the hall table under the piece of red granite where I keep the mail. Over the weekend we all went skiing, and time passed quickly.

But when he came home from school at noon on Monday, I could tell how disappointed he was. He spooned his soup around in circles, and picked at his sandwich, and for the first time I noticed how pale he looked. On Tuesday, because again there was no mail for him, I made him waffles for lunch. But even that failed to cheer him.

"Look, Richard," I told him, "have you looked in the newspapers? Did you see that picture of all the unsorted mail. A mountain of it. It's going to take longer than we thought."

"I guess so."

He kept waiting. Watching him, I observed for the first time the simplicity of his life, the almost utilitarian unrelieved separation of his time: school, home, sleep. Endless repetition. He needed a letter desperately.

On the weekend we skied again, scattering our energies on the snow-covered hills and coming home in the late afternoon.

Richard was so weighted with sleep that England must have seemed far away, indistinct and irrelevant, a point on a dream map.

But Monday morning he tells me he feels sick. His throat is sore, he says, and his head aches. I can hear an unfamiliar pitch of pleading in his voice, and know intuitively that he only wants to be here when the mail arrives. Martin is impatient and peers down his throat with a flashlight. "I can't see a thing," he says. "And his temperature is normal."

"He might as well stay home this morning," I say, "just in case he's coming down with something." (How expertly I carry off these small deceptions. And how instinctively I take the part of the deceiver.) Richard, listening to us debate his hypothetical sickness, looks at me gratefully. And humbly crawls back into bed to wait.

The mail comes at half-past ten. There is quite a lot for a Monday. Bills mostly, a letter from Martin's parents, two or three magazines. And a letter from England. A tissue-thin blue air letter. But it is from a friend of Martin's, not from Anita Spalding.

I go up to Richard's room, a tall glass of orange juice in my hand and an aspirin, for I want to continue the fiction of illness long enough for him to recover with grace.

"Take this, Rich," I say. "You may even feel up to going to school this afternoon."

"Maybe," he says. "Any mail?"

"Nothing much," I say, duplicating his nonchalance.

"Wonder if the mail's getting through from England," he speculates as though this were no more than an abstract topic.

"I think it is, Richard," I tell him quietly. "Dad got one this morning."

"Oh."

"But I suppose it will just trickle in at first."

"Probably."

"It may take another good week to clear it all."

"Yeah."

"How do you feel?"

"A little better," he says.

"Good," I say. "After lunch, how about if I drive you over to school?"

"Okay," he says.

But there was no mail for him that week or the next. The month was slipping by, and I still had not confronted Furlong. I weighed it in my mind, rehearsed it; I fortified myself, gathered my strength, prepared my grievances. Soon.

But there are other things to think of. Meredith will be seventeen on February twenty-seventh, and Martin suggests we all go to Antonio's for dinner. I fret briefly about the cost, but listening to my own voice and hearing the terse economical echoes of my mother, I stop short.

"A good idea," I say.

The day before her birthday I take the downtown bus and shop for a birthday present. This is a far different quest than shopping for my mother or for Lala; for them we can never think of anything to buy. But for Meredith, for a girl of seventeen, the shops are groaning with wonderful things. Things. It is the age for things, each of which would, I know, bring tears of delight rushing into her eyes. There are Greek bags woven in a shade of blue so subtle it defies description; chunks of stone, looking as though they were plucked from a strange planet, fastened into chains of palest silver; there are sweaters of unfathomable softness, belts in every colour and width, jeans by the hundreds, by the thousands, by the millions. Things are everywhere. All I have to do is choose.

But I can't. Instead I buy too much. I spend far more money than I'd intended; it is irresistible; it is so easy to bring her happiness — it won't always be this easy — so easy to produce the charge plate, to tuck yet another little bag away. But finally the parcels weight me down; my arms are filled, and I think it must be time for me to catch my bus. But first a cup of coffee.

In the corner of Christy's Coffee Shop I sink into a chair. The tables here are small, and the tile floor is awash with tracked-in snow; there is hardly room for me to stow my parcels under the table. At all the other little tables are shoppers, and like me they are weary. The February sales are on, and many of these women are guarding treasures they have spent the day pursuing. Waitresses bring them solace: cups of coffee, green pots of tea, doughnuts or toasted Danish buns, bran muffins with pats of butter. Outside it's already dark. Only four-thirty and the day is ending for these exhausted, sore-footed women. All of them are women, I notice.

Or almost all. There *is* one man at a table in the back of the room. Only one. Oddly enough, he looks familiar; the bulk of his body reminds me of someone I know. I do know him. I recognize the tweed overcoat. Of course. It's Furlong Eberhardt. With a cup of tea raised to his lips.

And who's that with him? Two women. Students? Probably. I peer over the sea of teased hairdos and crushed wool hats. Who is it?

One of them looks like Ruthie. What would Ruthie be doing here with Furlong? Impossible. But it is Ruthie. She is pouring herself a cup of tea, tipping the pot almost upside-down to get the last drop. She is lifting a sliver of lemon and squeezing it in. The small dark face, Latin-looking. It *is* Ruthie.

And who is that other girl? I can't believe it. But the navy blue coat thrown over the back of the chair is familiar. Its plaid lining is conclusive. The slender neck, the lift of dark brown hair. I am certain now. It is — yes — *it's Meredith!*

Every day I work for two or three hours on the Susanna Moodie biography. What I am looking for is the precise event which altered her from a rather priggish, faintly blue-stockinged but ardent young girl into a heavy, conventional, distressed, perpetually disapproving and sorrowing woman. And although I've been over all the resource material thoroughly, I'm unable to find the line of demarcation. It seems to be unrecorded, lodged perhaps in the years between her books, or else — and this seems more likely — wilfully suppressed, deliberately withheld.

There are traumatic events in her life to be sure. Illness. The drowning of a son which she mentions only in passing. Poverty. And the failure of her husband to assume direction. Perhaps that's it — her husband, John W. Dunbar Moodie.

There's a clue in an essay he wrote as

an old man. It is a sort of summary of his life in which he lists the primary events as being, one, getting stepped on by an elephant as a young man in South Africa, two, the breaking of a knee in middle life and, three, painful arthritis in old age. He was, it would seem, a man who measured his life by episodes of pain, a negative personality who might easily have extinguished the fire of love in Susanna.

But despite her various calamities she survived, and it seems to have been her sense of irony that kept her afloat when everything else failed. Over the years she had abandoned the sharp divisions between good and evil which had troubled her as a young woman; the two qualities became bridged with a fibrous rib of irony. Sharp on the tongue, it became her trademark.

Irony, it seems to me, is a curious quality, a sour pleasure. Observation which is acid-edged with knowledge. A double vision which allows pain to exist on the reverse side of pleasure. Neither vice nor virtue, it annihilated the dichotomy of her existence. Smoothed out the contradictions. Forstalled ennui and permitted survival. An anaesthetic for the frontier, but at the same time a drug to dull exhilaration.

For example, when Susanna was a middle-aged woman and ailing from unmentionable disorders, she took a cruise to see

Niagara Falls. It was, she says, what she had dreamed of all her life.

The imagined sight of that mountain of water had sustained her through her tragic years, and now at last the boat carried her closer and closer to the majestic sight.

She can hear the thunder of water before she can see it, and her whole body tenses for pleasure. But when she actually stands in the presence of the torrent, she loses the capacity for rhapsody. She has exhausted it in anticipation.

But irony rescues her from a pitiable vacuum. Turning from the scenery, she observes the human activity around her, and, paragraph by paragraph, she describes the reactions of her fellow tourists. Their multiple presence forms particles through which she can see, as through a prism, the glorious and legendary spectacle of Niagara Falls. Once again she finds her own way out.

I easily recognize the nuances of irony because, lying sleepless in bed on this last night in February, I too am rescued; I too do my balancing act between humour and desperation.

It seems I've always had a knack for it. Perhaps I was born with it; maybe it came sealed in the invisible skin of a chromosome, ready to accompany me for the rest of my life. I can feel it: a tough-as-a-tendon cord which stretches from the top of my head to my toes, a sort of auxiliary brain, ready as a knuckle to carry me through.

All through my endless barren childhood I had my special and privileged observation platform. My parents did not succeed in souring me as they did my sister Charleen who writes and publishes poems of terrifying bitterness. My sad lank father and my sad nervous mother have faded to snapshot proportions. They have not twisted or warped me or shaped me into a mocking image of themselves. There may be warnings in the blood, but, at least, there are no nightmares.

And now, in spite of my insomnia — that too is temporary — I find I'm able to coexist with Richard's agony as, day after day, the mail doesn't come for him. Somewhere in a larger pattern there's an explanation; I am confident of it.

And the complex dark secrecy of the scene in Christy's Coffee Shop — Furlong, Ruthie, Meredith — I can absorb that too, and I can even refrain from quizzing Meredith about it. I can put it aside, tuck it away; I can title it "An Anomaly."

Detached and nerved by irony, I can even look squarely at Furlong's devious theft. And at my own role as an agent of theft. I can live outside it. I can outline it with my magic pencil. Put a ring around it.

Martin's madness is more difficult to assimilate, but my vein, my good steady vein of irony, gives me just enough distance to believe he may be only temporarily deranged. And so, although everything seems to be falling apart and though I'm assailed by an unidentifiable sadness and though it has snowed solidly for eight days — there is one thing I am certain of: that, like Mrs. Moodie of Belleville, I will, in the end, be able to trick myself; I can will myself into happiness. No matter what happens I will be able to get through.

If only I can get through tonight.

March

"You swine, Furlong. You swine."

"Judith! Are you talking to me?"

"You thieving swine!"

"Judith, what is this? Some kind of joke?"

It is not a joke, not even a nightmare; this is real. At last I am confronting Furlong.

"Swine."

"Judith."

This isn't the way I'd planned it. But here we are, the two of us in the hall of Professor Stanley's country house with its pegged oak floors and its original pre-Confederation pine furniture and the acre of land which he and his wife Polly always refer to as "the grounds." We are face to face in front of the cherrywood armoire, and now that I have begun, I can't stop.

"Swine."

"Judith, are you serious? Are you calling me a swine?"

"That's exactly what I said. An evil swine."

"Come on, Judith." He steps back, half-shocked. And then enrages me further by allowing a curl of a smile to appear behind his beard.

Where had I got that word — swine? It is a word I haven't used since — since when? Since 1943 at least, since those fanatical early Forties, the war years, when the villains in our violent-hued comic books were resoundingly labelled swine by the hero, Captain Marvel, Superman, Captain Midnight, whoever it might be.

Swine meant the ultimate in the sinister, a being who was evil, whose skin was tinged with green and whose eyes were slits of gleaming, poisonous, rancid, incomprehensible Nazism. Japanese and Germans were swines (we didn't know how to pluralize it, of course), Hitler being the epitome of swinehood. It was a word we spit out between clenched teeth, saying it with a fiendish east European accent — "You feelthy schwine." When we jumped on tin cans at the school scrap drive we shouted, "Kill the swine."

I remember, years later, taking part in a school play called "The Princess and the Swineherd," and the term swine was explained to me for the first time. How disappointing to find that it meant no more than pig, for though I associated pigs with filth and gluttony, that animal didn't begin to approach the wickedness of swine.

"You heard me, Furlong. I said swine. And I meant swine."

"My dear girl, what on earth is the matter?"

198

"I am not your dear girl."

We are at a party, an annual get-together for the English Department, traditionally hosted by the department chairman and his wife, Ben and Polly Stanley.

I am fond of them both. Ben is reserved but charming, a specialist in Elizabethan literature, a man who at fifty seems perpetually surprised by his own dimensions. One hand is constantly rummaging through his coarse, silver-grey hair as though it cannot believe that such beautiful hair exists on so common a head. The other hand, nervously, mechanically, pats and circles the sloping paunch which bulges under his suede jacket, as if he is questioning its clandestine and demeaning swell.

His wife Polly is about fifty too, a woman both stout and shy. Sadly she is the victim of academic fiction, for she is never free of her role as faculty wife; she plays bridge with the wives, bowls with them, discusses Great Books with them, laments pollution, listens to string quartets, attends convocations, all with an air of brooding and bewilderment. Despite her girth, her charm is wispy, a fragile growth which advances and contracts in spasms. I would not want to embarrass her.

"I don't care if they hear us," I hiss.

"Well, damn it, I do."

As it happens, no one hears us. Everyone has gone into the wainscotted dining room for a buffet of clam chowder and the Stanley speciality, chunks of beef afloat in red wine, which they will carry on plates into the living room, the den, the solarium, anywhere they can find a perch. We are alone in the hall, Furlong and I, but nevertheless I lower my voice.

"Furlong, I want you to know that I know everything."

"You know everything," he repeats numbly. He is not smiling now.

"Everything."

"Everything," he echoes.

"You might have known I'd find out."

"I didn't. No, I didn't."

"How could you be so devious, Furlong?" I ask. Already I have passed from the peak of rage into vicious scolding.

He has the grace to cover his face with both hands, and I notice with satisfaction that he is swaying slightly.

"How could you be so deceitful?" I say again.

"Ah Judith." His hands extend in a gesture of helplessness. "This is all much more complicated than you seem to think."

"Complicated? Devious is more like it."

"Believe me, Judith, I never meant to hurt anyone."

"All you wanted was to watch out for

yourself and your precious reputation."

"You're wrong. There were other considerations. Really Judith, you're being unbelievably narrow-minded. And it's not like you."

"Please, please, please spare me any semblance of flattery, Furlong. I'm not in the mood."

"All I'm saying is, and for God's sake, lower your voice won't you, try to think of this in a broader perspective."

"Deception is deception," I say lamely but loudly.

"Believe me, Judith, I never meant for this to get out of hand."

"You admit then that it did get out of hand?"

"Of course I do. My God, do you think I've got no conscience at all?"

"I wonder about that."

"If you only knew. I've felt the most terrible remorse, believe me. I've been tormented day and night by all this. There were times when I thought I should go on television, on national television, and make a public confession."

"Well? Are you going to?"

He winces. Takes a step backwards. Raises his hand as though to ward me off. Sinks down on one of Polly's ladder-back chairs.

"Sit down. Please, Judith, we have got to

talk this over sensibly."

I sit facing him. My knees buckle with faintness. "We *are* talking this over, Furlong."

"Now listen closely, Judith. I am not defending what I did."

"I hope not."

"I am not bereft of honour, whatever you may choose to think."

"I wonder if you know what I really do think."

"I can guess. You are utterly disgusted. You trusted me, and now you find out what a sham I really am."

"You're getting close," I say cruelly.

"Do you know something, Judith. I even hate myself. When I look in the mirror I cringe. I actually cringe."

"You'd never guess it from the pitch on your book jackets."

"I don't write those, as you perfectly well know. The publishers look after that."

"I see."

"You don't see. You're being deliberately rigid, Judith, and I'm doing my best to explain to you the full circumstances."

"Go ahead. Try. I want to hear how you're going to explain this away."

"All right then." He takes a deep breath. "It seemed a harmless enough thing to do at the time. That's all. What more can I say. Perhaps I lacked perspective at the time. Yes, I definitely lacked a sense of balance. And then I just got trapped into it. Everything happened too fast. It just got away from me, that's all."

"And that's what you call an explanation?"

"It's not much. It's not much, I'll admit, but it's all I have. My God, Judith, you love to twist the knife when you get hold of it, don't you?"

"Well, I *am* the injured party."

"The injured party?"

"I'm the one you took advantage of."

"Why you?"

"For heaven's sake, Furlong, don't be obtuse. I can't stand that on top of all this rotten deception."

"I'm afraid I must be obtuse. I just fail to see why you are more injured than anyone else."

"You really can't?"

"No. I'm afraid not. I mean, all right, you're a member of the public. Maybe a little more astute than some, but you're just one member of a large public, and I can't see what gives you the right to be personally aggrieved."

I can't believe what I'm hearing. "Think, Furlong," I say, "think hard."

"I am. But I can't for the life of me think why you should feel persecuted."

"I can't stand this."

"You think I'm enjoying it. I came here

tonight expecting to enjoy myself, and I hardly get in the door and you leap on me."

"Believe me, I would have leapt a lot sooner than this, but I took a few weeks to cool off."

"And you call this being cool? If you don't mind my saying so, Judith, this really isn't your style, not at all. Pouncing on an old friend in public and yelling 'swine' at him."

"Well, you behaved like a swine, Furlong, and I don't see that you deserve any special consideration now."

"Didn't I tell you I was guilty. Do you want me to go down on my knees. And I really am sorry about it, Judith." His voice cracks, dangerously close to tears. "If you only knew what I go through. Do you know that I have to take sleeping pills almost every night. Not to mention my pre-ulcer condition."

"If that's the case, what in heaven's name made you do it?"

"I told you. I got trapped. It didn't seem so dreadful at the time. But listen Judith. You're an old friend. I know I acted like a bloody fool and that I've no right to ask this of you, but do you think we could — you know — do you think we could more or less keep this between ourselves? I mean, now that the damage is done, do we have to spread it around?"

"What you're really asking is, can we

sweep it neatly under the rug."

"Of course I don't mean that. I just mean, couldn't we confine this thing?"

"I don't know. I'll have to think."

"Judith. Please." His eyes fill with real tears and his nose reddens, making him look piercingly elderly. "Please."

I can't bear it; he is going to cry. "All right," I say grudgingly. "I suppose nothing would be served by a public disclosure."

"Oh, Judith, you are kind." He reaches blindly for my hand. "You've always been so kind, so good."

"But," I say firmly, drawing my hand away, "I do think you owe me, at the very least, an apology."

His face straightens; his eyes cloud with opaque bafflement. "Tell me, why do I owe you a *personal* apology?"

"It was, after all, my plot that you stole."

"Your plot. I stole your plot?"

"For *Graven Images*. As you perfectly well know."

"You think I stole a plot from you for *Graven Images*?"

"You certainly did. From my novel. The one I wrote for your class. And you promised me you'd destroyed it. And then you went and took it. Maybe not incident by incident, but the main idea. You took the main idea. And made a killing."

"Come, come, Judith. Writers don't steal

ideas. They abstract them from wherever they can. I never stole your idea."

"You must be joking, Furlong. Do you mean to sit there and tell me your novel bears no resemblance to the one I wrote?"

He answers with an airy wave of his hand, an affectionate pull at his beard. "Possibly, possibly. But, my good Lord, writers can't stake out territories. It's open season. A free range. One uses what one can find. One takes an idea and brings to it his own individual touch. His own quality. Enhances it. Develops it. Do you know there are only seven distinct plots in all of literature?"

"So you told us in creative writing class."

"Well, can't you see?" He is smiling now, suddenly sunny. "This is no more than a variation on one of those great primordial plots."

I am hopelessly confused. It is unbelievable that he should be sitting here beside me smiling. That he has shaken off every particle of guilt like an animal shaking water from his coat. My mouth is open; I am literally gasping for air; I cannot believe this.

"I'm sure you'll understand, Judith, when you take time to think about it."

My hands are shaking, and my mouth has gone slack and shapeless like a flap of canvas! I am unable to speak for a moment. Finally I sputter something, but even to me it is unintelligible.

"Ah, Judith, just think for a minute, where did Shakespeare — not that I am placing myself in that orbit for a second — but where did Shakespeare get his plots? Not from his own experience, you can be sure of that. I mean, who was he but another young lad from the provinces? He stole his plots, you would say, Judith. Borrowed them from the literature of the past, and no one damn well calls it theft. He took those old tried and true stories and hammered them into something that was his own."

"It's not the same," I manage to gasp.

"Judith, Judith, it is. Surely you can see that this is all a terrible misunderstanding."

I am numb. Is it all a misunderstanding? I try to think. But at that moment Polly Stanley, doing her hostess rounds, discovers us. "Oh, dear. I've been neglecting you two," she frets. "Here I am, about to serve dessert, and I don't believe you two have had a thing to eat."

"We were having a chat." Furlong beams. "Judith and I were discussing some old established literary traditions."

"Oh, dear, shop talk." She giggles faintly, but she is clearly annoyed that we have confused the progression of her dinner, and she takes Furlong firmly by the arm and leads him into the dining room. He goes off gratefully, and I follow behind them, mechanically filling a plate with food. The beef is rather cold; there is a dull skin of grease floating on top, but I load my plate anyway. Furlong hurries away to join a cheerful group in the solarium, and I am left.

Something is wrong. There is something I have not quite managed to assimilate. Furlong has declared his innocence. He has refused to accept a grain of guilt. He is emphatic; he is all sweet reason.

But then what in heaven's name have he and I been talking about?

"Judith."

"Yes." I am almost asleep. I had thought that Martin was asleep too.

"Why don't you come with me?"

"To Toronto?" I ask. Martin is leaving on the morning train for the Renaissance Society meeting.

"Why not come, Judith? Meredith could look after things here, and it would do you good to get away."

"I could never never be ready in time."

"We could take a later train."

"I don't know, Martin. Richard is so sort of depressed that I hate to leave him."

"Richard?"

"He still hasn't got a letter from England. What do you suppose has happened?"

"Oh, I wouldn't worry, Judith. Everything comes to an end eventually."

"I suppose so," I say.

I lie very still on my side of the bed. I am waiting for Martin to encourage me, to list the reasons why I should go to Toronto with him, and to brush aside my petty objections. I wait, believing that he will succeed in persuading me. I could wear my green skirt on the train; my long dress is back from the cleaners; I could have my hair done in Toronto; leave the rest of the ham for the children; phone them in the evening.

A street light shines into our bedroom from the place where the curtains don't quite meet, making a white streak down the bed. About two inches wide I estimate. It is very quiet. I can hear the Baby Ben ticking. Martin has set the alarm for six so he can make the early train.

Under the electric blanket I lie at attention. In a moment he will speak again, pressing me to go. But five minutes pass. I check the luminous dial of the clock. Ten minutes. I lift myself on one elbow to look at Martin.

He is very relaxed. His eyes are shut and he is breathing regularly, very deeply with a low diesel hum, and I notice that he is definitely asleep.

"Teen-agers are often sulky, resentful and hostile," writes Dr. Whittier Whitehorn in the second of a series of articles on adolescent behaviour. "And because they revolve so continuously around their own tempestuous emotions, they tend to interpret even the most general remarks as applying to themselves."

I read these newspaper articles less for their factual information than for the comfort of their familiar, kindly rhetoric. I know that Dr. Whitehorn can do no more in the end than counsel patience for "this difficult and trying emotional time," and I skip through the paragraphs to the closing line, noting with cheerful satisfaction that "in the battle to win a teen-ager's confidence, sensitivity and patience are the only weapons a wise parent can wield."

I let the newspaper fall to the floor, switch off the bedside lamp and try to sleep. When Martin is away the bed feels irrationally flat; I kick a leg out sideways, testing the space.

Dr. Whitehorn's advice glows in front of me as I review in my mind the strange, almost surreal discussion I had with Meredith this morning.

She had slept late, and at eight-twenty on a Monday morning she was still tearing through the house looking for her books.

"Do you have your bus tokens?" I asked her.

She answered with a short and heavy, "Yes, Mother."

"Your books?"

"No. I can't find *Graven Images*."

"What do you want with that?"

"I'm doing a report on it. For English."

"A report on *Graven Images*?"

"Why not?" she asked sharply. "Most people consider that it's quite good."

"It's in my room," I confessed.

"Do you mind if I take it?" she asked, elaborately polite now.

I replied with a tart, heavy-on-every-syllable voice, "Not in the least."

She whirled around, studied my face closely, and pronounced, "You really do have something against Furlong."

"I suppose."

"What?"

I shrug. "I just don't trust him."

"Why not?"

"I used to," I said, "but not anymore."

She was plainly alarmed at this. And hastened to his defence. "Look, Mother, I think I know what you're saying. About not trusting him. I mean, I know what you think."

"What?"

"I — I can't say anything. But just take my word for it that it's not true. It may look true at this moment but it isn't."

"What isn't?" I asked.

"That's all I can say. Just that it isn't true." And then with a touch of melodrama she added, "You'll just have to trust me."

"You'll miss your bus, Meredith," I said suddenly.

Why had I said that? Because it was all I could think of to say.

Now, Dr. Whitehorn, what do you make of that? Is that enigmatic enough for you? Perhaps I have remembered the conversation imperfectly. Or perhaps I have missed some of the underlying nuances, failed to exercise that sensitivity you're so big on. But why is my daughter talking in these tense, circular riddles? And why is it that I, her mother, can't understand her?

Nancy Krantz is a practising Roman Catholic, but she is also a believer in signs. Nothing so simple as horoscopes or palm reading; the signs she watches for and obeys are subtle and, to the casual eye, minuscule. She has come to rely on these small portents (a postage stamp upside-down, an icicle falling on the stroke of midnight, a name misspelled in the telephone book) but she is uneasy about admitting her faith in them. "If I confessed to sign-watching," she says, "I would be asked to name a Regulating Agent who sets up the signs and points the way." She prefers to see her omens as part of a system of electrical impulses which relate unlike objects, suggesting mysterious connections in another dimension of time. But admitting to such a belief, she says, leaves her open to charges of superstition or worse, marks her as a follower of the cult of intuition. Yet, she believes in signs and, furthermore, she believes that most other people do too.

Susanna Moodie, in one of her splendidly irrelevant asides, says much the same thing. "All who have ever trodden this earth, possessed of the powers of thought and reflection, have listened to voices of the soul and secretly acknowledged their power; but few, very few, have had the courage boldly to declare their belief in them."

And today I too have received a sign. Nothing flimsy like a dream, or mysterious like the surfacing of a familiar face: just a word, a single word, that started a chain reaction.

It began with a book by Kipling which Richard is reading for school. He hates it; it's dull, and he doesn't like the stylized way in which the characters speak. It is also rather long. Every night he brings it home from school, puts it on the front hall table, and in the morning he carries it back again, unopened. It is an old book from the school library. The binding is an alarming tatter of cloth and glue, and the dull-red cover is frayed around the edges. Its position on our hall table is becoming familiar, part of the landscape now; we expect it to be there. The lettering on the cover is shiny gold, and the title is curved along a golden hoop. Underneath it, curled the other way, is the name Rudyard Kipling.

Rudyard. Poor man to have such a strange name. Cruel Victorians to name their children so badly. I am struck by something half-remembered. Of course! Furlong's real name is Rudyard. His mother let it slip out once by mistake when she was talking to me. He never uses it, of course, and as far as I know no one else knows it. Rudyard. A secret name.

Secret. It hints at other secrets. Why is it I have kept this particular secret to myself? Why not? — it is a trifling fact — but it seems strange I've never mentioned it to Martin or to Roger.

Roger. Does Roger know about the name Rudyard? He did his Ph.D. thesis on Furlong. He is the authority on Furlong Eberhardt in this country; he cornered that little market about six years ago and stuffed it all into a thesis.

Thesis. Where is Roger's thesis? It is, without a doubt, where all doctoral theses are — on microfilm in the university library.

Library. What time does the library close? It's open all evening, of course. Until eleven o'clock. Martin is still in Toronto and I have the car.

The car. It is sitting outside on the snowy drive. The tank is full of gas and the keys are on the hall table. I can go. I can go this very minute.

Roger's thesis proved to be disappointing.

I had no trouble finding it. The librarian was helpful and polite: "Of course, Mrs. Gill. I'm sure we have Dr. Ramsay's thesis here." With her bracelet of keys she opened cupboards and pulled out metal drawers which were solidly filled with rows of neatly boxed microfilm. Hundreds of them. Each loaded with information which had been laboriously accumulated and assembled and then methodically stuffed away in these drawers where they were wonderfully, freely — almost, in fact, recklessly — available.

The films were arranged alphabetically, and it took only a few minutes before I found what I wanted: Ramsay, Roger R. — *Furlong Eberhardt and the Canadian Consciousness*. I yanked it out, electrified with happiness; it was so easy.

It took something like two hours to read it on the microfilm machine, but after the first hour I contented myself with skimming. For there was almost nothing of interest. And it was hard to believe that Roger with his fat yellow curls and Rabelaisian yelp of laughter could have produced this river of creamy musings. He had actually got past the examining committee with these long, elaborate, clustered generalizations, all artificially squeezed between Roman numerals and subdivided and re-subdivided until they reached the tiny fur of footnotes, appendices and, at last, something called the Author's Afterward? Hadn't someone along the line demanded something solid in the way of facts?

And the timidity, the equivocation — the use of hesitant pleading words like conjecture, hypothesis, probability — alternating with the brisk, combative, masculine "however" which introduced every second paragraph, as though Roger had been locked into debate with himself and losing badly.

His design, as outlined in the Preface, was to survey the texts of Furlong's first four novels, collate those themes and images which were specifically related to the national consciousness — which were, in short, definitively Canadian — all this in order to prove that Furlong Eberhardt more or less represented the "most nearly complete flowering of the national ethos in the middle decades of this century."

I had to remind myself that I hadn't come to carp at Roger's prose or even to question his ultimate purpose; I had come to unseal some of the mystery surrounding the person of Furlong Eberhardt. I had come for biographical material, and in that respect Roger's thesis was useless.

The explanation for the omission of personal data came in the Afterword in which Roger explained at length that in his study of Eberhardt he had attempted to follow the dictates of the New Criticism, a critical method which, he explained, eschewed the personality and beliefs of the author and connected instead on close textual analysis.

It was a disappointment. And it came as a surprise to me after spending a year and a half painfully abstracting the personality of Susanna Moodie from the rambling, discursive body of her writing, that anyone would deliberately set out to purify prose by obliterating the personality that had shaped it.

A paradox. I saw that I would have to find another way.

Thursday. I wake up early remembering that this is the day Martin is to make his presentation to the Renaissance Society.

When I drove him to the train on Monday

I noticed that, in addition to his battered canvas weekender, he was carrying a heavy cardboard carton to which he had attached a rough rope handle. His woven tapestries must be packed inside, although he didn't mention them to me. Were they finished, I wondered. How had they turned out? How would he display them? But because they seemed to represent something obscurely humiliating, I kept silent. The subject of the *Paradise Lost* weavings had been so assiduously avoided by both of us, that I felt a last-minute plea on my part to abandon the presentation would be ridiculous.

So I said nothing; only kissed him and told him I would meet his train on Friday night, and watched him walk toward the train in a wet sludgy snow, carrying the shameful suitcase, a ludicrous umbrella from Birmingham days, and the damning cardboard box that banged against his leg as he climbed aboard, set on his lunatic journey. Oh, Martin!

This morning at ten o'clock he is scheduled to give his talk and presentation. I have seen the conference program which says "Dr. Martin Gill — *Paradise Lost* in a Pictorial Presentation." I will have to keep busy; I will have to make this day disappear.

It strikes me that I might as well continue my pursuit of information regarding Furlong. So after lunch I go to the big downtown library.

Granite pillars, crouched lions, the majestic stone entrance stairs covered with sisal matting and boards for five months of the year (what a strange country we live in!), a foyer imperial with vaulting, echoes, brass plaques, oil portraits, uniformed guards, a ponderous check-out desk and on it, purring and whirring, the latest in photostatic machines. Two librarians, tightly permed, one fat, one thin, stand behind the desk. The card catalogue snakes back and forth in a room of its own; surely I will find something here.

I carry books to a table, check indexes, cross-check references, try various biographical dictionaries and local histories, and conclude after several hours that Furlong had done a remarkable job of obscuring his past. He seems hardly to have existed before 1952 when his first book was published. I do find two passing references to a Rudyard Eberhart in the Forties; the surname is misspelled and the geographical location is wrong; they are cryptic notations which I don't really understand but which I nevertheless make note of. I will have to go to the Archives if I am to discover anything more. Another day.

This is the library where Ruthie St. Pierre

works, and as I put on my coat and scarf, I think that it would be nice to stop and have a chat with her.

Her office is on the top floor, a tiny glassed-in cubicle in the Translation Department. I climb the stairs and go past a maze of other tiny offices.

And then I glimpse her through the wall of glass. She is bending over a filing cabinet in the corner and she is wearing a pantsuit of daffodil yellow and platform shoes of prodigious thickness. She finds what she wants, straightens up and turns back to her desk.

And I would have knocked on the glass, I would have gone in and embraced her and told her how much I had missed her all winter (for I *had* missed her) and told her how morose and sullen and seedy Roger is looking and how he doesn't even know where she is living or how she is getting along — but I don't go in because I can see plainly that she is in the seventh, perhaps eighth, and who knows — she is such a tiny girl — maybe even the ninth month of blooming, swelling, flowering pregnancy.

I watch her for a moment to be sure, to be absolutely certain, and then, quickly and quietly, I make my retreat.

Afterwards, driving home, I can't understand why I had left her like that. It was a shock, of course, and then too I hadn't wanted to create what for Ruthie might be a painful and embarrassing meeting. Certainly she had gone out of her way to avoid friends all winter.

When I was sick with the flu she had sent a basket of fruit — not ordinary apples and oranges, but wonderful and exotic mangoes, kiwifruit, red bananas, passion fruit, figs and pomegranates, and I had written her a thank-you note, mailing it to the library where she works. Once in the following weeks she had phoned to see if I was better. "I'm fine now, Ruthie," I had said, "but how are you?"

"Fine, Jude, fine." (She is the only person in the world who consistently calls me Jude.) "I guess you know that Roger and I have called it quits."

"Well," I said uneasily, "yes, and I'm sorry."

"It's all for the best. Roger's not one for settling down, you know. Look, Jude, I've got to go. The big boss is prowling today. Bye for now. Keep the faith."

"You too," I said, not knowing which faith she referred to, but sensing that she had meant: respect my privacy, leave me alone for a while, ask me no questions, hold off, give me time, keep faith in me.

So I hadn't phoned her again, and today I hadn't rushed into the little office. But later I wished I had. She had looked both brave and fragile in her yellow suit, and I had been moved by the gallantry with which she concentrated on her filing cabinet, pencil in hand, and that enormous abdomen bunching up in front of her.

I am late getting home from the library. It is dinner time, and Richard suggests we send out for a pizza.

When it arrives Meredith and Richard and I eat it in the family room, along with glasses of ginger ale. The curtains are pulled and the television is on. It gets late and I should send the children to bed; I should remind them that this is a school night, but I am reluctant to break up our warm, shared drowsiness. Ruthie is far away now, as far away as a character in a story — did I really see her? Furlong Eberhardt seems foreign and trifling — what matters is our essential clutter of warmth and food and noise.

Eleven o'clock. The news comes on. More Watergate, more Belfast, another provincial land scandal, and then, to wind up the news, a lighter item. Dr. Martin Gill is introduced. Unbelievably his face spreads across the screen.

There is not a sound from us. The three of us, Meredith and Richard and I, do not speak; we do not even move; we are frozen into place.

The interviewer explains that Dr. Gill has startled both the art and the literary world by creating — he consults his notes — a graphic presentation of *Paradise Lost* (a famous seventeenth century poem, he explains to all of us out in TV land). Presented today at a national symposium on literature, it was a tremendous sensation. Two art galleries have already made impressive bids for the tapestries. "Is that true, Professor Gill?" the interviewer asks.

The camera goes back to Martin. "Yes, it does appear to be true," he says with engaging modesty.

The interviewer continues with a long information-packed question, "In that case, it would seem that this work of yours, quite apart from the interest in connection with the poem, has an intrinsic, that is, a beauty of its own."

"I am really quite overwhelmed by the response," Martin says, his slow, slow smile beaming out across the country. Beautiful. It is a highly individual smile, both provocative and sensual — I've never noticed that before.

The two faces fade, giving way to sports and weather, and the children and I slowly turn to look at each other. Richard and Meredith are staring at me and their mouths hang open with awe. And so, I perceive, does mine.

And then we leap and dance around the room; singing, shouting, laughing, hugging each other. We order another pizza, a large special combination. Friends phone to ask if we've seen Martin, and we phone Martin several times at his hotel and finally, at two o'clock in the morning, we reach him and talk and talk and then dizzy, crazy, mad with happiness we go stunned to bed.

In the morning there are three things for me to read. First the Toronto newspaper — a write-up on Martin and a picture of him posing in front of the weavings. I peer intently at the tapestry but, as in most newsphotos; it is smeary and porous and not very effective. Martin though, with his nice white teeth open in a smile, comes out very well.

PROFESSOR WEDS ART TO LITERATURE

English professor Martin Gill delighted his colleagues at the Renaissance Society yesterday with a change from the usual staid academic papers. His presentation was a pictorial representation of *Paradise Lost*, Milton's famous epic masterpiece. Using the techniques of tapestry making, Dr.

Gill, a distinguished scholar, used different colours to represent the themes in the poem, and produced not only a visual commentary on the piece, but a stunning work of abstract art. Three art galleries, including the National Gallery, have placed bids for the work.

The idea was intended as a teaching aid, Dr. Gill explained. "The poem is so complex and so enormous that often the student of Literature loses the total Miltonic pattern."

Dr. Gill is the son of Professor Enos Gill of McGill University, author of *Two Times a Nation*. His wife is Judith Gill, the biographer. About the feature Dr. Gill denies that he will divorce literature for art. "It's only been a temporary romance," he said to reporters with a chuckle. "I wouldn't trust my luck twice."

Next I read a note from Furlong. I had been expecting this, knowing that once he realized he had tipped his hand, he would make haste to smooth over the traces.

My dear Judith,

I'm sure you regret as much as I our little misunderstanding the other night. I must say I was more than usually rattled by your startling lunge at my throat, and I'm afraid I lost what the youth of today would call my cool. No doubt I babbled like a complete looney. As soon as I realized what it was that concerned you — I refer to your mistaken impression that I had appropriated your plot for *Graven Images* — I came to my senses, and can only hope that you came to yours as well. Judith, my pet, we have been good friends for too long to allow this misunderstanding to come between us. The truth is, I value your friendship and, yes, I admit it, perhaps I did get a new slant from your aborted novel, but as I explained to you, writers are no more than scavengers and assemblers of lies. You have done me a good turn; perhaps I may be able to do the same for you one day.

Fondly,
FURLONG

Last of all I read an airletter from England. At first, seeing the bright blue paper and feeling the familiar featherweight paper, I thought that Anita Spalding had finally come through. But no, it is addressed to us, to Dr. and Mrs. Martin Gill.

Dear Dr. and Mrs. Gill,

First of all let me thank you for your very kind Christmas card. I apologize for the silence from this end. I will be passing quite near you in a month's time, and if it is not too terribly inconvenient, might I call on you? I will be in New York for a few days conferring with my publisher (I am about to have a novel published) and there is an item of some urgency which I am anxious to discuss with you. In addition, I am most desirous of making your acquaintance. Please do not go to any trouble for me. I shall be in the city only two nights (I have already secured hotel accommodation) and I should be distraught if my sudden appearance were in any way to inconvenience you.

> I remain,
> Your obedient servant,
> JOHN SPALDING

P.S. We have had a nasty winter compounded by strikes and fuel shortages, not to mention my own distressing personal affairs. I trust all is well with you and your family.

> JS

April

I wake early one morning. Something is amiss. A wet smell. What is it? I sniff and instead of the usual hot metal smell of the furnace, I smell something different.

And I hear something. Water running. Someone has left a tap on all night. "Martin," I say. "Are you awake?"

"No," he says crossly. "It's only six-thirty."

"What's that sound, Martin?"

"I can't hear anything."

"Listen. It's water dripping. Can you hear it?"

He listens for a minute. "I think it's just the snow melting," he says. "It's the snow on the roof."

I listen again. It *is* the snow; it's running off the roof in rivulets. It's pouring through the downspout.

And that explains the funny smell. It's the grey-scented, rare and delicate-as-a-thread smell of the melt. Spring.

At last.

Hurriedly I write a letter to John Spalding.

Dear John, *(I use his first name, avail-*

ing myself of the North American right to be familiar.)

We were delighted to get your letter and look forward to seeing you at the end of the month. Are you sure you wouldn't like to change your plans and stay with us? We have plenty of room and would enjoy having you. Martin and I are anxious to know if you are bringing your wife and daughter. All of us, and especially Richard, of course, would love to meet them. If this note reaches you before you leave England, do drop us a line and let us know.

Our congratulations to you on the publication of your novel. We look forward to hearing more about it.

Sincerely,
JUDITH GILL

(And then because no letter to or from Britain seems complete without a reference to the weather, I add —) P.S. We have had a long winter and lots of snow, but spring is on the way now, and by the time you arrive the last of the snow will be gone.

JUDITH

In a week I had a reply.

Dear Judith, *(Aha, familiarity is contagious.)*

Thank you for your kind offer of a bed which I accept with gratitude. As for my wife, she and I have recently separated. Isabel has returned to Cyprus and has taken Anita with her. I supposed — wrongly I see — that Anita had written to your son about the chain of events. But then she has not even written to me very regularly. All this is rather upsetting to her, no doubt. Her mother has attached herself to a rogue of a gigolo, a cretinous beach ornament, and Anita has no doubt seen more of the unsavoury world in the last month than is good for her. The whole subject is exceedingly painful to me at the moment; thus, perhaps it is for the best that you know before I come.

There are daffodils blooming all over Birmingham. Truly glorious.

> Best wishes,
> JOHN SPALDING

Isabel Spalding gone off with gigolo! I picture him, heavy with grease, cunningly light-fingered and handsome. And her, pale and sluttish in a bikini. Poor Anita.

I hasten to tell Richard about what has

happened in far-off Cyprus. For although the correspondence may be ended, it is better for him to know that there is, at least, an explanation; he has not been rejected; he has not accidentally written something offensive, he has not been the victim of a love that was unrequited.

I explained to him how traumatic a sudden shift in geography can be to a child, not to mention the catastrophic splintering of a family. He nods; he can understand that. Later she may feel like writing, I tell him. Yes, he says, perhaps. I gaze at him, trying to think of something further to comfort him, but he dashes away saying, it doesn't matter, it doesn't matter. Does he mean it? He has survived this long.

BUFFET SUPPER
WHERE — *62 Beaver Place*
WHEN — *April 30th, 8:00*
Judith and Martin Gill

We are going to have a party. Or, as my mother would say, we are going to entertain. Not that entertaining was something she ever did. Only something she would like to have done. She would love to entertain, she always said, if only the slipcovers were finished, if only the lampshade was replaced, if only Bert — our father and her husband — would fix the cracked piece of tiling in the bathroom. She would entertain if she had more room, if the children were older and off her hands, if chicken weren't so expensive, if her nerves didn't act up when she got over-tired.

But she never did. Only her sister and a few close relatives and neighbours ever sipped coffee at our kitchen table. Mrs. Christianson, Loretta Bruce who lived across the street in a bungalow identical to ours, which my mother always said needed some imagination as well as some spit and polish, a Mrs. McAbee; timid women, all of them, who flattered our mother on her "taste," who asked, when they had finished their Nescafé, well, what have you been doing to the house lately? Then she would lead them into the living room, or bedroom or whatever, and point out the new needlepoint cushion or the magazine rack with its felt appliqué, and they would chorus again how clever she was. Poor swindled souls, believing that women expressed their personalities through their houses. A waste. But maybe they really thought differently.

The buffet supper was Martin's idea. "We have to do something with him," he said when he read John Spalding's letter. "Besides we haven't had a party since December."

I make up a list of people. About thirty

seems right. Nancy and Paul Krantz, the Parks and the Beerbalms from the neighbourhood. And some university people. Furlong? I can't decide what to do with him, first thinking that nothing could persuade me to have him, the traitor, the thief, the liar. But it is unthinkable, on the other hand, to exclude him. Besides, I might have a chance to ask him a few searching questions. But then, I argue, why should I invite him, especially after that self-serving note he sent me in which he cast me in the role of a crazy woman who lunged and who took easy neurotic offence, and himself as the worldly artist, just self-depreciating enough to admit to minor dishonesties. Swine. But I had to invite him. For one thing, Mrs. Eberhardt must be invited, for I could depend on her to draw out John Spalding, should he turn out to be someone who needed drawing out.

And what about Ruthie? Should I invite her? She would probably refuse, but just what if she didn't? I decided to consult Roger, so I phoned him at his office.

"Roger," I said, "we're having a party. Martin and I. In a couple of weeks."

"Terrific."

"John Spalding is coming from England. Remember hearing about him?"

"Sure. Your old landlord."

"Right. Well, I'm writing invitations and

I wonder if — well — I'd like to invite Ruthie, of course, but I don't want to put either of you on the spot."

"Ruthie," he mused.

"Just tell me what you think, Roger. Shall I ask her or not?"

A pause. And then he said, "Sure. I suppose we can't avoid each other forever. Not in a city this size."

"Okay then," I said. "Ruthie's on the list. I'll have to send this to her at the library I suppose. Or have you discovered where she's living?"

Another pause. Longer this time. "Well, yes. I guess I do know where she's living."

"Really? Where?"

"This may sound odd, Judith, but it seems she is staying at the Eberhardts' apartment."

I am surprised. Very surprised. "At Furlong's? Ruthie is staying at Furlong's?"

"Yeah."

"Are you sure?"

"Sure I'm sure."

"How'd you find out?"

"Well," he paused again, "the truth is — I guess I should come right out with it — the truth is I followed her home one night. From the library."

"And she went to Furlong's?"

"Yes. Amazing isn't it. I couldn't believe it at first, so the next night I followed her again. Same time. Same place."

Cunningly I asked, "How did she look, Roger? I mean — is she okay?"

"Fine, as far as I could tell, fine. It was fairly dark, of course. I'd love to say she was thin and pinched and lonely looking, but actually she looked quite okay. I think she's even put on some weight."

"Really?"

"Yes. And, of course, when I thought it over, it isn't all that extraordinary you know. Her staying there. They were always good to both of us, both Furlong and his mother. Sort of adopted us. And God knows she's safe enough with Furlong. As you well know."

"Roger. This is sort of a personal question and you don't have to answer if you don't want to."

"What is it, Judith?"

"Why is it you and Ruthie never got married?"

"I had a feeling you were going to ask that. Well, the answer is that Ruthie never wanted to get tied down."

"That's funny."

"Why?"

"Because she once said the same thing about you. That you didn't want to get tied down."

"I suppose we both spouted a lot of nonsense."

"Do you suppose things would have worked out if you had been married?"

"I suppose. I mean, it makes it a little more difficult to split if you've got all that legal mess."

"Is it really over then, Roger? With you and Ruthie? Not that it's any of my business."

"I'd hate to think so. I think she just needs time on her own. To sort things out. Get her head together."

I had been sympathetic to this point, but suddenly I was enraged. "Damn it, Roger. Damn it, damn it."

He sounded alarmed. "Judith, what have I said?"

"All that blather about getting heads together."

"It's just an expression. It means —"

"I know what it means. But it's so — so impossibly puerile. Do you think anyone ever gets it all sorted out? Gets it all tidied up, purged out, all the odds and ends stowed away on the right shelves? Do you really believe that, Roger?"

"Sometimes you need time. How can you think in a thicket?"

"That thicket happens to be a form of protection. It's thinking in a vacuum that's unreal."

"Judith, I just don't know," he sighed. "I just don't know anymore."

"Look, Roger, I think I'll just send this

invitation to Ruthie's office. I don't want her to know that I know where she's staying if it's such a big mystery."

"Good idea."

"She probably won't come anyway."

"Probably not," he said dolefully.

I am putting the finishing touches on Susanna Moodie. In the mornings I go over the chapters one by one, trying to look at her objectively. Does she live, breathe, take definite shape? Is the vein of personality strong enough to bridge the episodes? The disturbing change in personality: it bothers me. Dare I suggest hormone imbalance? Psychological scarring? It's unwise to do more than suggest. I'm not a psychologist or a doctor, as the critics will be quick to point out. But I do have a feeling about her. I wonder though, have I conveyed that feeling?

Aside from her two books about life in Canada, Susanna Moodie wrote a string of trashy novels, potboilers really, limp-wristed romances containing such melodramatics as last minute rescues at the gallows and death-bed conversions and always, unfailingly, oceans and oceans of tears. She was desperate for money, of course, so she wrote quickly and she wrote for a popular audience, the Harlequin nurse stories of her day.

But one of the books she wrote has been invaluable to me. It is a novel entitled *Flora Lindsay* or *Episodes in an Eventful Life*. Astonishingly, it is Susanna's own story, or at least an idealized picture of it, an autobiography in fictional form. The heroine, Flora, is like Susanna married to a veteran of the Napoleonic Wars. Like Susanna, Flora and her husband (also named John) emigrate to Canada. Even the ship they sail on bears the same name, the *Anne*. Like Susanna, Flora has a baby daughter and, like her again, she has employed an unwed mother as a nurse for her child.

Thus, by watching Flora, I am able to see Susanna as a young woman. But, of course, it isn't really Susanna; it's only a projection, a view of herself. Flora is refined, virtuous, bright, lively, humorous; her only fault is an occasional pout when her husband places some sort of restraint on her. Did Susanna really see herself that way?

How do I view myself? — large, loose, baroque. Compulsively garrulous, hugely tactless, given to blurts, heavy foot in heavy mouth. Fearsome with energy, Brobdingnagian voice, everything of such vastness that my photographs always surprise me by their relatively normal proportions — ah, but that's only my public self. And Mar-

tin, does he view himself — now flushed with victory from the Renaissance Society — as a cocky counterculture academic? Does he carry a newsreel in his head with himself as maverick star, a composed and witty generalist who nimbly leaps from discipline to discipline, who proved his wife wrong about the whole concept of poetry portrayed in wool, but resists saying I told you so? Just smiles at her his slow and knowing smile and thinks his secret thoughts, maybe wondering how he would look with long hair and that ultimate obscenity on middle-aged men, beads?

Susanna wrote *Flora Lindsay* when she was a middle-aged woman, and she had by that time suffered repeated trials, many births, several deaths, unbearable homesickness and alienation, not to mention a searing lack of intellectual nourishment. Looking back, she may have viewed that early life, that time of high expectations and simple married love as a period of comfort and happiness, seeing herself as the nimble and graceful heroine, not the prudish, rather shallow and condescending woman she more than likely was. She was so shrewd about her fellow Canadians that she enraged them, but nevertheless seemed to have had little real understanding of herself. Is it any wonder then, I ask myself

as I send the manuscript off to a typist —
is it any wonder that I don't understand
her?

"Why hello, Mrs. Gill."

"Judith! Long time no see."

"What can we do for you today, Mrs. Gill?"

They know me at the Public Archives.
I've spent hours and hours in these shiny
corridors working on my biographical research, exploring filing cabinets, pulling
out envelopes, and going through the con-
tents, sometimes finding what I need, but
just as often not. And always I am
astonished at the sheer volume of trivia
which is being watched over.

The librarians guard their treasures dili-
gently, and they are unfailingly kind in
their willingness to spend an hour, sometimes two or three, finding the origin of a
single fact. But today I don't need any help.
I am quite sure I can find what I want.

Name and year: Furlong Eberhardt (possibly Rudyard Eberhart). As for dates, I
work backwards from the present.

It takes longer than I think. A clue, tan-
talizing, leads nowhere, and I spend an
hour in a cul-de-sac; just when I think I'm
finding my way out, the reference turns
out to apply to someone else. I press my
hands to my head. Exhaustion. What am
I doing here?

In the cafeteria I have a bowl of soup

and a sandwich, and later in the afternoon I get lucky. One reference leads to another; I skip from drawer to drawer, putting the pieces together. And they fit, they fit! I have it. Or almost. I'll have to check at the Immigration Department, but I know what they'll say. I am already positive.

It's this: Furlong Eberhardt, Canadian prairie novelist, the man who is said to embody the ethos of the nation, is an American!

I want to hug the fact, to chew on it, to pull it out when I choose so I can admire its shiny ironic contours and ponder the wonderful, dark, moist, hilarious secrecy of it.

Rudyard Eberhart, born Maple Bluffs, Iowa, only son of Elizabeth Eberhart, widow.

Eligible for draft in 1949 (Korean War), left Maple Bluffs the day notice was delivered.

Landed immigrant status (with mother) in Saskatchewan.

Attended U. of Sask., was once written up in local paper as grand loser (shortest fish) in a fishing competition.

Began writing short stories under the name of Red Eberhart. Gradual shift to Eberhardt spelling, finalized with publication of first novel, 1952.

Christened Furlong by a kindly critic, after which he travelled from strength to strength until arrival at present eminence.

Ah, Furlong, you crafty devil.

I could not remember being so wonderfully amused by anything in all my life. My throat pricked continuously with wanting to laugh, and for the first few days it was all I could do to keep the corners of my mouth from turning up at inappropriate moments, so amused was I by the spectacle of Furlong Eberhardt who, with scarcely a break in stride, traded Maple Bluffs for the Maple Leaf; marvellous!

But in my delight I recognized something which was faintly hysterical, something suspiciously akin to relief. What had I expected to find? That Furlong had his novels written for him by a West Coast syndicate? That he might be guilty of a crime more heinous (murder? blackmail?) than mere trifling with the facts of his private life? That something unbearably sordid had poisoned his previous existence? Yes, I had been badly frightened; I admitted it to myself.

Poor Furlong. I could see it all: how he had — I recalled his own words — got into it innocently enough and then was unable to extricate himself, taking a free ride on the band wagon of nationalism and unable to jump off. Well, don't worry, Furlong, I won't betray you now.

Poor Furlong, so eager to be accepted, to be loved.

Poor Furlong, suffering in miserable and ageing secrecy.

Poor Furlong. Dear Furlong.

"Martin," I whisper after the lights are out, "what do you think of John Spalding?"

Pause. "He seems okay," Martin says. "Not quite the nut I expected."

"Me either. Where did I get the idea he was going to be short?"

"And fat! Christ, he's actually obese. Cheerful guy though."

"Shhhhh. He's only one thin wall away."

"Never mind. He should be dead to the world after those three brandies he tucked away."

"Did you ask him about his wife? While I was making coffee?"

"Good God, no. What would you have me say, Judith? 'Sorry to hear you've been made a cuckold, old man.' "

"Did you at least mention that we were having a party tomorrow night?"

"Yes."

"What did he say?"

"Just sort of rumbled on about how he

hoped we weren't going to any trouble for him."

"He certainly is different than what I expected. It's a good thing we had him paged at the airport or we'd never have found him."

"Funny, but he said the same thing about us."

"What?"

"That he wouldn't have recognized us in a thousand years. He had us pictured differently."

"Really? I wonder what he thought we were like."

"I didn't ask him."

"I would have."

"You would have, Judith, yes."

"It might have been interesting. Don't you ever wonder, Martin, how you look to other people? The general impression, I mean."

"No," he said. "To be truthful, I don't think I ever do."

"That's abnormal."

"Are you sure?"

"No. Maybe it's abnormal the other way. But still I would have asked him."

I turn to look at Martin. The street light shining into our room and neatly bisecting our bed, permits me to study him. He is lying on his back, relaxed with his hands locked behind his head. And on his face I see a lazy, enigmatic smile. I peer at him intently.

"Why are you smiling, Martin?"

"Me? Am I smiling?"

"You know you are."

"I suppose I was just thinking foul and filthy midnight thoughts."

"About?"

He runs a hand under my nightgown. Stops in the slope between my thighs.

"Sshhhhhh," I say. "He'll hear us."

"Fuck him."

"Well, that's a switch."

"Shhhhhhhh."

Nancy Krantz came a little early to give me a hand with the party.

Martin and Paul Krantz and John Spalding drank gin tonics in the living room, and she and I flicked dust bits out of wine glasses with paper towels, heated pots of lasagna and cut up onions for the salad. My party menus (like my décor, my hair style, my legally married status) are ten years out of date; I know that elsewhere women, prettier than I and wearing gowns of enormous haute daring, are serving tiny Viennese pancakes stuffed with herring, or scampi à la Shanghai, but I willingly, willfully, shut my eyes to all of that.

Nancy, larky and ironic, takes note of our female busy work; contrasts us to the booze swillers in the next room, lolling in chairs, dense in discussion. She is in violent good cheer, dextrous with the stacks of plates and cutlery, ingenious with the table napkins, setting out candles in startling asymmetrical arrangements, never for an instant leaving off her social commentary. "Parties are irrational but necessary. Where are the extra ashtrays, Judith? If you set aside those parties which are merely chic, which exist just for the sake of existence, then there is something biblical and compelling about raining down a lot of food and drink on a lot of people gathered under a single roof at an appointed hour. Almost the fulfillment of a rite. And it brings on a sort of catharsis if it really works. And why not? You've got an artificial selection of people. The personalities and the conditions are imposed. A sort of preordered confrontation. I thought you had one of those hot tray things, Judith."

"I do. Now where did I put it last time I used it?"

She finds it on the top shelf above the refrigerator, polishes it briefly, plugs it in. Ready to go.

Roger is the first to arrive. "I know I'm early," he apologizes, "but I wonder if — you know — is Ruthie coming? Or not?"

"Not," I tell him. "She phoned to say she'd like to come but couldn't make it."

"Why not?" he says, flinching visibly.

"She didn't say."

"Oh, Jesus," he says. "I knew it."

"Come on, Roger. I want you to meet John Spalding. He's in the living room."

"Oh yeah," he says. And whispers, "What's he like?"

"I don't know. I've hardly seen him. He slept until noon and had an appointment this afternoon. We haven't had too much time to talk to him."

"Nice guy?"

"Nice enough," I say. "But I'd stay off the topic of faithless women. He's in the midst, so to speak."

"Righto," he says, disappearing into the living room.

After that things get busy. The doorbell rings continuously it seems, and since it is raining heavily outside, I am occupied with finding places for boots while Richard ferries dripping umbrellas to the basement and Meredith hangs raincoats upstairs on the shower rail.

From the living room, the family room and even the kitchen there is a rising tide of noise, stemming at first from polite muted corners, erupting then into explosive contagious laughter, passing through furniture, through walls, melding with the mingled reverberations of wood, china, cutlery, a woman's shrill scream of surprise.

Bodies are everywhere, slung on couches, chair arms, kitchen counters; I have to move two people aside to find room to set the casseroles down.

Our parties are always like this, a blur from the first doorbell to the last nightcap — fetching, carrying, greeting, serving, clearing, scraping, rinsing, smiling hard through it all, wondering why I ever thought it was going to be a good idea, and yet exhilarated to fever pitch and this on barely half a glass of wine.

I am at the centre of a hurricane, the eye of calm in the middle of ferocious whirling circles. Between the kitchen and hall I pause, trying to sense the pattern. What has become of John Spalding, guest of honour whom I have introduced to absolutely no one? Ah, but Martin has looked after him. There he is in the exact centre of the beige sofa, plumply settled with a brimming glass, a woman on either side of him and Polly Stanley, awkward but surprisingly girlish, on the floor at his feet. All are laughing; I can't actually hear them laughing, not over all this noise, but they are locked into laughing position, heads back, teeth bared.

Mrs. Eberhardt is sitting in our most comfortable chair doing what she was invited to do, drawing out quieter guests and being charming and kindly and solid; she is the oldest person in the room. By far the oldest. Does she mind? Does she even notice?

Ben Stanley and Roger have their heads very close together near the fireplace; they look vaguely theatrical as though they had selected this location to accent the seriousness of their discussion. I can tell from the confidential tilt of their heads that they are on the subject of departmental politics. Roger is mainly listening and nodding as befits his junior status. Besides he is apolitical; power doesn't interest him yet.

From far away I hear the telephone briefly pierce the hubbub. Two rings and someone answers it. Someone's baby sitter probably. No, it's for Furlong. Meredith goes to find him. She discovers him refilling a plate with salad, and she whispers lengthily into his ear. I can see them talking. Meredith is distraught; her hands are waving a little wildly. Furlong puts down his plate and hurries off to the phone where he talks for some time, cupping his hand to shut out the noise. After that I am too busy to watch.

Someone knocks over a glass of wine. I wipe it up. I set out cream and sugar on the table. Check the coffee. Someone arrives late and I find him some scrapings of lasagna and a heap of wilted salad. But later, serving plates of chocolate torte, I see that Meredith and Furlong are again conferring earnestly in a corner. After a moment they motion to Roger to join them, and the three of them huddle together. Furlong is explaining something to Roger who is leaning backwards, stunned, shaking his head, I don't believe it, I don't believe it.

"How about some dessert?" I break in on them.

There is a sudden catch of silence. Embarrassment. Uncertainty. A fraction of a second only. Then Furlong takes my hand gently, "Judith, you must forgive me, but I'm afraid I'll have to leave early. Something unexpected has come up."

"Nothing serious?" I ask, for I'm suddenly alarmed by their shared gravity.

"No. Not exactly."

"You'd better tell her," Meredith directs.

"Perhaps I'd better."

"I wish to Jesus someone had told me," Roger says, half-sullen, half-violent.

"What's happened?" I demand.

"It's Ruthie." Furlong says her name with surprising tenderness.

"Ruthie?"

"I don't suppose you know, but she is — well — expecting a baby."

"Yes, I did know, as a matter of fact."

"I *knew* you suspected something," Meredith says ringingly.

"Why didn't you tell me, Judith?" Roger charges. "You never said a word to me about it."

"I've only known for a few weeks. I saw her. At the library. She didn't see me, but I saw her. I haven't told anyone. Except Martin, of course."

"You could have phoned me. One lousy phone call."

"Look, Roger," Furlong says, "Ruthie didn't want you to know. That was the point."

"I have a right to know. Who has a better right?"

"Well now you know."

"How did *you* find out, Meredith?" I ask.

"I met her one day. A couple months ago. Downtown after school. Furlong had just taken her to the doctor. They sort of had to tell me. I mean, it was pretty obvious."

"Anyway, Judith," Furlong breaks in, "that was Ruthie on the phone a few minutes ago."

"Don't tell me —"

"Yes. At least she thinks so. She's had a few twinges."

"But it's not supposed to be for another two weeks," Meredith says.

"What kind of twinges?" I ask Furlong.

"I don't know. That is, I didn't ask her

what sort. Baby twinges, I presume."

"How far apart?"

"I didn't ask her that either."

"I'm surprised," I can't resist chiding him. "All those women in your books who die of childbirth. I would think you'd at least ask how far apart the pains are."

"Twenty minutes," Meredith interrupts. "I asked her."

"Christ. Twenty minutes." Roger moans.

"I think I'd better be going," Furlong says. "She's all by herself. She's been staying with Mother and me for the last little while."

"Yes. I think you'd better go too," I say. "And you'd better hurry. It could be quick."

"Jesus." Roger yells.

"Why don't you go too, Roger?" I say.

Furlong nods. "Maybe he should."

"What about me?" Meredith pleads. "Can't I come too?"

Furlong glances at me. I nod.

"The three of us then," Furlong says. "Mother can get a taxi later. I'll just have a word with her on the way out."

In a moment they are gone, and no one has even noticed their leaving. The wall of noise encloses me again; the volume after midnight doubles, trebles. In the living room I hear singing: "There's a bright golden haze on the meadow." Someone is rolling up the rug; someone else has found

Meredith's rock records.

Unexpectedly I come across Richard who is carrying towers of coffee cups into the kitchen. As he passes I reach out automatically to pat the top of his head. The springy spaniel hair is familiar enough, but there is something different. My hand angles oddly; can it be that he's grown this much?

He shouts something into my ear. What is it? "Great party, Mother," he seems to be saying. Or something like that.

Finally they go home, the last guest disappears into the rain-creased darkness, the last car swerves around the corner of Beaver Place where all the other houses are dark. It's after three.

Martin carries a pot of tea into the wreckage of the living room, three cups on a tray, milk and sugar, a fan of spoons. "Sit down, Judith," he commands.

John Spalding, boulder-like, is still occupying the middle of the sofa. Has he moved all evening, I wonder?

At this hour we abandon the last remnant of formality. I kick off my silver shoes, note where the straps have bitten into the instep, and put my stockinged feet on the coffee table. Martin pours tea and hands me a cup.

"John," he says, "surely you'd like some too."

"Please," he booms from the cushions.

We sip in silence, letting the quiet wash over us.

Martin inquires about John's plane. It leaves at ten-thirty, a mere seven hours away. Martin has an early appointment, so it is decided that I will drive John to the airport.

"I hope the noise wasn't too much for you tonight," I say.

"Not in the least. I enjoyed it all. My first glimpse of North American informality. Spontaneous and delightful."

"I'm sorry your visit has been so short," I tell him. "We've hardly had a chance to get acquainted." He waves aside my remarks with a plump hand. "I feel I've got to know you well just by staying with you."

"Perhaps you'll be back this way before long," Martin says politely. "Seeing publishers and so forth."

"When exactly is your novel coming out?" I ask.

"In about a month's time," he says. "And that reminds me, there was a little something I wanted to mention to you both." He looks around the room, glances at his watch and says, "That is, if it's not too late for you?"

"Oh, no," I say. "It's not too late for us. Is it, Martin?"

"No, of course not," Martin says wearily.

"Well, the fact is," John Spalding says,

making an effort to sit up straight, "the fact is that this isn't the first novel I've written."

"Really?" I say brightly. Too brightly?

"The truth is I've written several. But none of them was ever published. I never seemed to hit on an idea worth developing. Until a year or so ago."

"Yes?" Martin and I chorus.

"Finally I struck on something workable. And I owe the idea for my novel to you. To your family that is."

"To us."

"You see, I have, in a matter of speaking, borrowed the situation of your family. A Canadian family who spend a year in England."

"Your novel is about us?" Martin asks incredulously.

"Oh, no no no no. Not really about you, not exactly about you. Just the situation. A professor on sabbatical leave comes to an English university in an English city."

"Birmingham?"

"Well, yes. But I'm calling it Flyxton-on-Stoke. They have two children —"

"A boy and a girl?"

"Right. You've got the picture."

"But," Martin says, setting down his cup, "I suppose the resemblance ends there."

"Almost," John Spalding says, smiling a little nervously. "You may find a few other trifling similarities. That was why I wanted to mention this to you. So that when you read it, if you read it, you won't think I've — well — plagiarized from real life. If such a thing is possible."

"But how did you know anything about us?" I ask.

He laces his fingers across his broad stomach and, settling back, says, "Firstly, one can tell something about people simply by the fact that they have occupied the same quarters."

I nod, thinking of the bag of lightbulbs in the Birmingham bathroom, the sex manual under the mattress. Not to mention the shelf of manuscripts.

"Then there were the letters," he continues.

"But we never wrote you any," Martin says. "The university arranged the letting of the flat."

"No no no no no. I mean Anita's letters. The letters which your son Richard, a fine boy by the way, wrote to our daughter."

"You read the letters?"

"Good Lord yes. We all quite looked forward to them. Anita used to read them aloud to us after tea. Ah, those were happier days. He writes a fine letter, your lad."

Martin and I exchange looks of amazement. "And your novel is based on Richard's letters?"

"Oh, no no no no. Again he fills the air with a spray of little no's like the exhaust from a car. "I didn't exactly *base* the novel on it. Just got a general idea of the sort of people you were, how you responded to things. That sort of thing."

"And you just took off from there?"

He beamed. "Exactly, exactly. But I did want you to know. I mean, in case you had any objections."

"It seems it's too late for objections even if we did have some," Martin says dryly.

"Well, yes, that is more or less the case. But you see, a writer must —"

"Get his material where he can find it," I finish for him.

"Quite. Quite. Exactly. And, of course, I have changed all the names entirely."

"What are we called?" I ask eagerly.

"You, I have called Gillian. Martin is simply inverted to Gilbert Martin."

"Very clever," Martin says, tight-lipped.

"We'll look forward to reading it," I say. "Will you send us a copy?"

"You may be sure of that. And I'm more than pleased that you seem to understand the situation."

"What I can't understand," Martin says, "is how you could find material for a novel out of our rather ordinary domestic situation. I mean, what in Christ did Richard write you about?"

"Yes what?" I ask.

John Spalding opens his mouth to speak, but we are interrupted by someone banging on the back door.

Martin rises muttering, "Who on earth?"

"Oh," I suddenly remember. "It's Meredith. I completely forgot about her."

"Meredith! I thought she was in bed hours ago. What's she doing out at three in the morning?"

She's standing before us, a raincoat over her long patchwork dress, her hair clinging siren-like to her slender neck. Her face is shiny with rain, but more than that, it is iridescent with happiness, and she says over and over again as though she can't quite believe it, "It's a boy. It's a boy, seven pounds, ten ounces, a beautiful, beautiful baby boy."

May

It is the morning after our party, the first morning in May.

"I know what you think," Meredith charges, "and it isn't true."

"What isn't true?" I ask. I am cleaning up after the party, putting away glasses, trays, and casseroles that won't be needed again. Until the next time.

"About Ruthie's baby."

"What about Ruthie's baby?"

"I'm just saying that I know it looks suspicious. With Ruthie living at the Eberhardts' and all that. But it really isn't the way it looks."

"Meredith!" I face her. "You've got to make yourself clear. What is the awful thing that you suspect me of suspecting?"

"I know you've had doubts. I can tell by the way you talked about Furlong."

"And how exactly did I talk about Furlong?"

"You said you didn't trust him. Remember? You didn't trust him anymore."

"Well, that may be true."

"But if you'd only listen to me for a minute, I'm trying to tell you that it wasn't

Furlong at all."

"What wasn't Furlong?"

Meredith sighs and with enormous deliberation pronounces, "Furlong is not the father of Ruthie's baby."

"But, Meredith, I never thought he was."

"You didn't?" she says, her voice draining away.

"No, not for a minute."

"But —"

"Whatever gave you that idea?"

She flounders. "I just thought — well here was Ruthie, big as a barn — and living with Furlong — what else could you possibly think?"

"Well, I never once thought of Furlong. You can be sure of that."

"But why not?"

Can it be that she doesn't realize about Furlong? Must I tell her? "Meredith," I say, "don't you know that Furlong — well — surely you must have noticed — I mean, I just wouldn't ever suspect Furlong of anything like that. It's just not the sort of thing he would do. At all."

For some reason she has started to cry a little, and, sniffling, she says, "I thought for sure you thought it was Furlong."

"No, Meredith, no," I tell her. "Never for a moment. Truly."

She reaches blindly for a Kleenex, blows her nose and looks at me wetly, smiling somewhat foolishly, and I am struck, not for the first time, by her unique blend of innocence and knowledge; a curious imbalance which may never be perfectly corrected; out of stubborn perversity she wills it not to be, conjuring a guilelessness which is deliberate and which perhaps propitiates life's darker offerings. Always at such moments she reminds me of someone, someone half-recalled but never quite brought into focus. I can never think who it is. But today I see for the first time who it is she reminds me of: it's me.

Now that the warmer weather is here to stay, Richard and his friends are outside most of the time. Baseball has taken possession of him, but not only baseball. His disappearances are often long and unexplained, and his comings and goings marked only by the banging of the back door.

Lately the phone rings for him often, school friends, kids in the neighbourhood, and one day there is someone who sounds almost girl-like.

It is a girl. His startled blush confirms it. She begins to phone fairly often — her name is Maureen — and sometimes he talks to her for an hour or more. About what? I don't know because he speaks in his brand-new low-register voice and cups his hand carefully over the receiver. And says nothing to us.

But he is suddenly happy again. I knew, of course, that it would come, knew that he was too young and resilient to be slain by the death of a single love. Martin told me he would get over it. And I knew all along that he would.

But I never dreamed it would be this; something so simple, something so natural.

And so soon.

"Living meanly is the greatest sin," Nancy Krantz tells me. "Needless economy. It thins the blood. Cuts out the heart."

It is so warm this morning that we have carried our coffee cups out on the back porch. "What about thrift?" I ask her.

"A vice," she says, "but an okay vice. Thrift, after all, implies its own raison d'être. But cheapness for its own sake is destructive."

We swap frugality stories.

She tells me about a man, a lawyer, well-to-do, with a beautiful house in Montreal, a summer place in the Rideau, annual excursions to London, the whole picture. And whenever he wanted to buy any new clothes, where do you think he went? You'll never guess. Down to the Salvation Army outlet. He'd pick through piles of old clothes until he'd find a forty-four medium. And that's what he wore. Pinstripe suits with shiny elbows. Navy blue blazers faded across the shoulders. Pants that bagged at the knees. Fuzzy along the pockets. He just didn't care. He'd take them home with him in a shopping bag and then he'd put them on and look at himself in the mirror. And he'd say, "Well, I'm no fashion plate but it only cost me three and a half bucks."

"Terrible, terrible," I breathe.

And I tell her about a widow, not wealthy, not even well-to-do, but not poverty-stricken either. She owns her own house, has an adequate pension and so on. But she had to have a breast removed, a terrible operation, she suffered terribly, cancer, and after she was discharged from the hospital she took the subway home. The subway! With a great white bandage where her left breast had been. On the subway.

"That's awful," Nancy says in a shocked whisper.

"But," I tell her, "that's not the worst part."

"What could be worse than that?" she asks.

I hesitate. For Nancy who is my good, my best friend, has never been an intimate. But I tell her anyway. The really awful thing was that the woman with the sheared-off breast riding home on the subway was my own mother.

"Oh, Judith, oh, Judith," she says. "Why didn't I tell you?"

"Tell me what?"

She gives a short harsh laugh. "That the man with the second-hand suits — was my father."

After that we sit quietly, finishing our coffee not talking much.

What have we said? Nothing much. But we have, for a minute, transcended abstractions. Have made a sort of pledge, a grim refusal to be stunned by the accidents of genes or the stopped-up world of others. We can outdistance any sorrow; what is it anyway but another abstraction, a stirring of air.

Although Ruthie no longer believes in the Catholic Church, or in marriage for that matter, she and Roger have asked a priest to officiate at their wedding. Not a priestly priest, Roger tells us. Father Claude is young and liberal-leaning, attached in some nebulous way to the university; his theology is aligned with scholarship rather than myth; he is a good guy.

Both Roger and Ruthie want to have the ceremony out-of-doors, but this proves difficult to arrange. A hitherto unknown by-law prohibits weddings in city parks. And going outside the city involves a procession of cars, which is aesthetically unacceptable to them. And, besides, what if it rains?

They ask us if they can have the wedding in our back yard. At first I protest that our yard is too ordinary for a wedding, having nothing to offer but a stretch of brownish grass, a strip of tulips by the garage, a few bushes, and a fence.

"Please," they say, "it will be fine."

And it is fine. The sunshine is a little thin, but there's no wind to speak of; for the middle of May it's a chilly but reasonable afternoon. The boys next door agree to carry on their ball game at the far end of the street, so it's fairly quiet except for an occasional thrust of birdsong. Best of all, the shrubs are in their first, pale-green budding.

Ruthie wears a long, wide-yoked dress printed with a million yellow flowers, and Roger arrives in that comic costume of formality, a borrowed navy blue suit.

There are no more than fifteen guests, a few friends of Ruthie's from the library, Furlong and his mother (in purple crimplene and mink stole), a friend of Roger's who makes guitars, a gentle couple (he batiks, she crochets) who live in the flat beneath them. Ruthie has not invited her parents; they would not feel comfortable at this type of wedding, she thinks.

She and Roger and Father Claude stand

near the forsythia, and the rest of us wait, shivering slightly, in a circle around them. Ruthie, who has been taking a night course in jewelry making, has made the rings herself out of twisted strands of silver. Roger has written the wedding service which, surprisingly, is composed in blank verse. "For you, Martin," he says. "I want you to be able to speak your part to a familiar rhythm."

We all have parts which we read from the Xeroxed scripts Roger has prepared; even Richard and Meredith have a few lines. I read:

> *Let peace descend upon this happy day*
> *That Man and Woman may with con-*
>   *science clear*
> *Respect each other yet remain themselves*
> *Their first commitment to the inner voice.*

(A dog barks somewhere, a delivery van whines around the bend in the road; a few neighbourhood children peer hypnotized through the fence.)

After the exchange of rings, Meredith fetches the baby from the pram (our wedding gift) which has been parked in a spray of sun near the garage. Bundled in a blanket, he is brought forward and christened Roger St. Pierre Martin Ramsay, a name lushly weighted with establishment echoes.

Roger loves it: "Listen to that roll of r's," he says. "Pure poetry."

A friend of Ruthie's sits cross-legged on the grass and plays something mournful on an alto recorder, and then we go into the house to drink Roger's homemade wine and eat the plates of exotic fruit which Ruthie has brought. And a surprise: Meredith has made a beautiful multi-layered cake topped with flowers, beads and sea shells. Why sea shells? "For fertility," she deadpans.

The afternoon drains away, leaving us steeped in a pale, translucent peace, relaxed, very much at our ease, talking quietly, content, but it occurs to me finally that there is a distinct lack of festivity. Something is missing from this gathering. It's joyous enough, but it's contained and diminished in some way. At first — out there in the garden — I had felt something more, something trying to come into being. Perhaps it was those heavy iambic lines we uttered or the sombreness of the recorder music, but there is no fine edge of nerve in this marriage rite, no undercurrent, no sense of beginning or expectation. Why?

I look at the bridal pair. Ruthie rocks little Roger St. Pierre while big Roger leans over them, bottle in hand, anxiously testing it against his wrist. Ruthie looks up at him, and what passes between them is a look of resignation, a little tired already, an arc of strain so subtle I think afterwards that I may have imagined it.

At five the baby begins to cry, and Roger and Ruthie go home. Everything has been fine, just as they said it would be. Just fine. I want to rush after them and tell them: everything will be just fine.

Near the end of the term the English Department has a dinner. As always it is held at the Faculty Club, and as always we eat thinly sliced roast beef, mashed potatoes, peas, and, for dessert, molded ice cream.

Whoever arranges these things, Polly Stanley probably, has placed me next to Furlong. (I have only this morning received a communication from the Citizenship Branch informing me that one Rudyard Eberhart was made a Canadian citizen in a private ceremony two years ago.)

"Well, well, Judith," he says. "How is Susanna Moodie these days?"

"About to go to the publishers," I tell him. "The typist has it now."

"And did you do it this time, Judith? Did you really wrap it up?"

I sense his genuine interest. And am oddly grateful for it. "No, not really," I admit. "I have a few hunches. About the real

Susanna. But I can't quite pin it all down."

"You mean she never came right out and admitted much that was personal?"

"Hardly ever. I had to look at her through layers and layers of affectation."

"Such as?"

"Oh, the gentle lady pose. The Wordsworthian nature lover. And the good Christian mother. She's in there somewhere, lost under all the gauze."

"Perhaps," he suggests, "all those layers act as a magnifying glass."

"How do you mean, Furlong?"

"Simply that instead of obscuring her personality, they may pinpoint her true self. Those particles of light which are allowed to escape, and I assume she occasionally emitted a few, can be interpreted in a wider sense. In a way it's easier than sorting through buckets and buckets of personal revelations."

"If I'd only been allowed five minutes with her," I tell him. "Five minutes, and I could have wrapped it up."

"I don't know, Judith. Perhaps you're expecting too much. People must be preserved with their mysteries intact. Otherwise, it's not real."

"Do you really believe that?"

"From my soul."

"Can I take that as a particle of light?"

"You may."

"Well, next time I'm going to write about someone still living. So I can get those five minutes."

"Who is it to be?"

"I'm not sure," I tell him. Then I smile and say, "Maybe I'll do you, Furlong."

I have startled him; he isn't sure whether or not I'm serious. "Surely you're joking?" he asks.

"Why not, Furlong? You're an established writer. Your life story might make fascinating reading."

"It wouldn't, it wouldn't, I assure you. And besides I'm not nearly old enough to have a biography written about me."

"Lots of younger people have been done. We could title it *A Biography Thus Far.* That sort of thing."

"Judith, you're not serious about this?" He is genuinely alarmed now.

"Wouldn't you like it?" I ask teasingly.

"Absolutely not. I prohibit it. I'm sure I have that right. I refuse permission, Judith."

"But I never asked."

"Judith, you know perfectly well you can't write about a living subject if he objects."

"But you're famous. You're in the public domain."

"It doesn't matter. Now Judith, tell me you're not serious."

I tell him. "I'm not serious, Furlong. I was only joking."

"Fine, fine." He relaxes, goes back to his ice cream. "And now let's talk about something interesting. Tell me what Martin has up his sleeve for the next Renaissance Society meeting. Tell me what you're planning for the summer. Tell me about the children. That's a lovely dress you're wearing. And isn't your hair different? Tell me, Judith. Tell me anything."

Any day now John Spalding's book will be out. *Alien Interlude* it's called, and when I think about it, my breath hardens in my chest. We are about to be revealed to ourselves. It's a little frightening.

Martin and I have decided not to tell Richard about the book and the fact that he was unwittingly the provider of material. For one thing it would make a mockery of his own jealous secrecy, and he might, with reason, look upon it as an act of treachery.

Martin and I, a little nervously, await our promised autographed copy. "Chances are," Martin tells me, "we won't even recognize ourselves. Remember what he told me when we met him at the airport? That we didn't remotely fulfil his image of us."

"And he didn't look the way we had pictured him either," I add. "Which proves something."

"Besides, writers use material selectively."

"Right."

"And another thing, Judith, I have a feeling that John Spalding is given to wild hyperbole."

"What do you mean?"

"Remember the famous Cyprus beachboy who carried his Jezebel-Isabel away?"

"Yes?"

"Just before the party, when he and I and Paul were talking about Cyprus, he happened to mention that when they were there his wife had been rushed into hospital one night for an emergency appendectomy. And while she was there she fell in love with her doctor. It turns out the gigolo he wrote us about, is also chief surgeon in a Nicosia hospital."

"I see," I say slowly.

"Not quite the penniless, suntanned seducer we were led to believe."

"Interesting," I say.

And though I don't tell Martin, I too have reasons to believe we may not recognize ourselves in *Alien Interlude*. I have seen how facts are transmuted as they travel through a series of hands; our family situation seen through the eyes of preadolescent Richard and translated into his awkward letter-writing prose, then crossing cultures and read by a child we have never seen, to a family we have never met, then mixed with the neurotic creative juices of John Spalding and filtered through a publisher — surely by the time it reaches print, the least dram of truth will be drained away.

And there is something more. When I drove John Spalding to the airport, I brought up the subject of Furlong Eberhardt and his book *Graven Images*. "Have you read it, by any chance?" I asked him.

"Curiously enough," he answered, "I did read it. Stuffy prose. But a ripping good yarn I thought."

Astonishing. He hadn't recognized his own plot which had passed first through my hands and then into Furlong's. More fuel for the comforting fire.

Martin says we'll probably get a good laugh out of the whole thing. Maybe. Maybe not.

Anyway, we're waiting.

With true capitalistic finesse, Martin has sold his tapestries of *Paradise Lost* to the highest bidder, an anonymous private collector; for us it is a sizable sum.

And with true middle-class flair, we have used the sum to lighten our mortgage, a fact that depresses us somewhat. Have we no imagination?

"Let's at least go out to a good dinner," Martin says. "Let's go to the revolving restaurant."

It has another name — something French and chic, but in this city it is always known as the revolving restaurant. We've not been there before, although it was constructed more than two years ago. It is expensive, we've been told, and quiet with subdued lighting and intimate tables; the food is rumoured to be good but routinely international, running from shrimp Newburg to steak Diane. Nothing unexpected. Just a nice evening out.

When we arrive at eight o'clock for dinner, having carefully made reservations, the restaurant is almost deserted. "That seems odd," I say to Martin. "Hardly anyone here."

"It's Monday night," he reminds me. "Probably pretty slow early in the week."

"Why are we whispering?" I say over the tiny table.

"I don't know," he whispers back.

There is another whispering couple next to us, and a short distance away is a party of eight. But, strangely enough, they aren't talking at all. I don't understand it.

But when the waiter comes to light our little claret-tinted hurricane lamp and my eyes become focused, I see what it is that is so puzzling about the group of eight: they are a party of deaf-mutes.

Their hands wave madly in the half-dark, making shadows on the walls, and their heads bob and dip over their shrimp cocktails.

The unreality of the scene enthralls me. I order mechanically — mushrooms à la grecque and pepper steak. Salad? Yes, Thousand Island please. Martin orders a bottle of wine, but I hardly notice what he's asked for. I am watching the delicate opening and closing of those sixteen hands.

Their animation is apparent, and that is what is so startling, for it is an animation which is associated with voices, with sounds, with noise. And from this circle of people, this circle of delicately gesturing hands, fringed and anxious as the petals of an exotic flower, comes a cloud of perfect, shapely silence.

They are eating their salad now. They indicate to the waiter the type of dressing they prefer, and something amuses them. Their faces break, not into laughter, but into the positions of laughter, the shapes, curves and angles of mirth. It is not quite real.

One of them has chosen filet of sole which the waiter expertly bones at a side table. This leads to a mad flurry of wrists and flying fingers, takes the shapes of birds, flowers, butterflies, the rapid opening and closing of space, shaping a private alphabet of air.

They are drinking wine, several bottles and, though it does not loosen their tongues, they grow garrulous; their hands fly so fast that they have hardly a moment to take up their knives and forks and, by the time they eat their desert, Martin and I have caught up with them.

There are three women and five men, all about the same age, in their late thirties probably. It must be a club, and this, perhaps, is their end-of-season wind-up.

What does the waiter think as he hands them their Black Forest cake and fresh strawberries? Will he knock off work tonight happier than usual? Sail home in the knowledge that he has shared in a unique festival of silence? Will he climb into bed with his wife and tell her how they pointed out their choices on the menu, how they were never still for a moment, how they, with consummate skill and, yes, grace, communicated even over the final coffee and liqueurs?

Martin watches them too. But for him it is no more than picturesque. A charming scene. He will remember it, but not for long.

For me it's different. I am expanded by the surreal and passionate language of their speechlessness. Their gathered presence enlarges me; we revolve together through the lit-up night. I can imagine them parting from each other after this evening is over, boarding their buses or taxis and branching out to their separate destinations, trailing their silence behind them like caterpillar silk. I can see them producing keys from pockets, opening doors, and entering the larger stories of their separate lives.

I am watching. My own life will never be enough for me. It is a congenital condition, my only, only disease in an otherwise lucky life. I am a watcher, an outsider whether I like it or not, and I'm stuck with the dangers that go along with it. And the rewards.

They are rising from the table now. Shaking hands. Exchanging through their fluttering fingers a few final remarks. A benediction. I am watching them, and out of the corner of my eye I see Martin watching — not them — but me. He has no need of the bizarre. What he needs is something infinitely more complex: what he needs is my possession of that need. I am translator to him, reporter of visions he can't see for himself.

Though I can't be sure even of that. Furlong may be right about embracing others along with their mysteries. Distance. Otherness. Martin's wrist on the table: it hums with a separate and private energy.

But I note, at least, the certainties, the

framework, the fact that he will shortly add up the bill, overtip about 5 per cent, smile at me from across the table and say, "Ready, Judith?"

And I, of course, will smile back and say: "Yes."

Carol Shields' critically acclaimed novel *The Stone Diaries* won the 1995 Pulitzer Prize for Fiction. *The Stone Diaries* also won the National Book Critics Circle Award and the Governor General's Award of Canada as well as being nominated for the Booker Prize. Her other books include *Happenstance*, *The Republic of Love*, *Swann*, *The Orange Fish*, and *Various Miracles*. *Small Ceremonies* won the Canadian Authors' Association Award for Fiction. Shields was born in Chicago and now lives in Winnipeg.

We hope you have enjoyed this Large Print book. Other G.K. Hall & Co. or Chivers Press Large Print books are available at your library or directly from the publishers.

For more information about current and upcoming titles, please call or write, without obligation, to:

G.K. Hall & Co.
P.O. Box 159
Thorndike, Maine 04986
USA
Tel. (800) 223-2336

OR

Chivers Press Limited
Windsor Bridge Road
Bath BA2 3AX
England
Tel. (0225) 335336

All our Large Print titles are designed for easy reading, and all our books are made to last.